BILL BRADSHAW

DELPHINE

Some boxes are best left closed

MAESTEI
PRESS

Copyright © 2020 by Bill Bradshaw/Maester Press
All rights reserved. This book or any portion thereof
may not be reproduced or used in any manner whatsoever
without the express written permission of the publisher
except for the use of brief quotations in a book review.

First Printing, 2020

ISBN 978-1-5272-6712-1

Maester Press
Lisdoonvarna, County Clare
Republic of Ireland

www.maesterpress.ie

Edited by: DavidShires.com
Formatting by: Novel-Development.com
Cover design by: TheImageDesigns.com

'In Memory of Noel Tolan - An Officer and a Gentleman.'

For Jack

For Ger

For Tik

A very special thanks to David R Shires, The Image Designs and the good people at Maester Press. Thanks also to Ian Murphy, Sheila Murphy, Shane Kelly, Morgan Vance, Fiona Clark, Grazia Kasak, Nancy Phillips and John 'The General' Pitts.

About the author:

Bill Bradshaw wrote the bestselling novels *'From the Horse's Mouth - A Jailer's Tale (2004)'* and, more recently, *'Hello Welcome (2017)'* which won a Book of the Month award in Los Angeles and Book of the Year award for 2018. He wrote, produced and directed the multi award winning short film *'The Long Night Followed'* which earned him a Best Writer award in New York. He lives on the west coast of Ireland where he drinks spiced rum and scribbles. He is currently working on a new book.

Prologue:

    Chapter 1: Whispers
    Chapter 2: Way Back When
    Chapter 3: Delphine
    Chapter 4: On Flanders Field
    Chapter 5: Back To The Front
    Chapter 6: All The Fallen Angels
    Chapter 7: Lifting The Veil
    Chapter 8: As God Intended
    Chapter 9: The Last Waltz
    Chapter 10: A Family Reunion

Epilogue:

PROLOGUE:

There are places that haunt our memory ... winding roads that stray from the path ... old houses where the winter wind whistles through cracked glass and forgotten hallways ... rooms that harbour our secrets. They follow us in the shadows. We can grow up, even grow away, but the ghosts of our past still reach out and take us to those hidden places. Burrows so bleak, so unholy that even God himself dare not enter. Come the morning light, we are reduced to children and we rise to face the day with an uneasiness that sits badly with who we think we are.

But what becomes of us if that new day never comes? What if the night conjures up a loathing, a violation, a monstrosity that would seize us from the sunlight? There is a veil that hangs between this world and the next. It keeps us apart till death says otherwise but, of course, there are no absolutes. The fabric becomes frayed from time to time and, if a force is powerful enough, demented enough, it can tear its way through.

Sometimes it's a strength borne from loss, a tragedy that must play itself out but sometimes the power is so black, so wickedly perverse that it cannot be contained by one realm or the other. This entity is hell-bent on destruction and it knows no mercy. It feeds on fear and pain...and it feeds often. It's known by many names ... Move Lespri in Old Creole ... Zmey in ancient Macedonia

DELPHINE

... Duh rău in Romanian folklore ... Kutsal Olmayan in Turkey ... Moloch ... the Iblis, cast out by God himself.

This is a presence that breeds contempt, an evil that corrupts and devours. Its depravity knows no equal and it cares little that you accept its existence or not for it changes nothing. Ignorance and scepticism are the planes it flourishes on and it seeps through the cracks until it lines the contours of a just man's soul ... and makes it unjust ... an abomination. This is how it reaches out to the world.

CHAPTER ONE: WHISPERS

'Fear and Guilt are sisters'
Shiley Jackson - US Author

The house on Kilchoman Road had been neglected for quite some time. That's not to say it hadn't been lived in. Eileen Brady had stayed there right up to the time the good folks at St Gabriel's came to liberate her from her solitude. But she had grown frail and fractured there over the years and, by the time they stretchered her out, the house had become a mirror for the illness that had fed off her bones.

It had never been a welcoming place, at least not in the memory of those who had grown up around it, and the stories that had been handed down meant that the old lady's isolation was somehow acceptable to the community. Fear can justify many things... even cruelty and neglect... but, of course, the building and its inhabitants were no strangers to either so they were best not discussed. People got about their business, time passed and Eileen Brady was condemned to drift deeper into the dark.

Town records would show that the house had occupied that plot since the dying days of the 19th century and the lake, to its rear, may have lent itself to family outings were it not for its history. It was a place best left to itself and, in hindsight, so it should have been. Peter Casey had been the Brady family solicitor as his father had been before him. It was a duty handed down to him and not one he volunteered for.

Saying that, he fulfilled his commitments to Eileen and, when she left for the nursing home, he made every effort to maintain the dwelling until it could be disposed of on her demise.

Although Drumasheen had little to offer in the way of excitement, it was nestled between the nearby west coast towns of Kilchoman, which sported the ruins of several Celtic forts and Kilbriggan, which had a notable golf course that attracted weekenders. The town itself had an occasional horse fair to cater for a small gypsy community and there was a crumbling prison on its outskirts that had seen a violent and tragic upheaval back in the 90's. There were those who suggested the towns' negativity had seeped from the very bricks that built the Brady household and they lamented that the great fire of '69 had not consumed it entirely. But it was not to be and, that the building had survived all these years was merely a further indication of its enduring quest to cast a shadow on the town-land of Drumasheen. Peter Casey would not be swayed by superstition. It wasn't that the stories surrounding the house were in anyway trite to him, he knew more than most of its dark history, but his logic wouldn't allow the past to impede on the present and he had a job to do. When Eileen was finally moved, he had some minor renovations carried out and, once the painters had finished, he advertised the place as 'a breakaway haven....a West coast retreat' in the regional newspapers of the East.

When a Dubliner called Markham booked for a week that following summer, Peter hoped that this would spirit in a brighter and, indeed, more lucrative era for the property.

Markham arrived from Dublin with his daughter, Katie, in June of that year. He explained that his wife would be joining them the following day and Peter engaged him in small talk about the virtues of the West. When it came time to hand over the keys, however, Casey felt a pang that left him uneasy. He watched Katie as she buzzed about his secretary regaling her with stories of life in the capital and overflowing with the nervous excitement of embarking on Secondary school later in the autumn. There was a sense of deja vu that he found deeply unsettling and he was not alone in that concern. His secretary stared passed the girl as Peter produced the keys and he felt that there was a judgement in her glare. He shook it off, as solicitors do, and the deal was done. When the Markhams had gone, Casey's secretary asked if she might step outside for a while but she did not go far. He saw her through the office window as she stood on the street in silence and watched the Markham's car drive into the distance.

Jack Markham had just cooked his first country meal and they were browsing through a *'Things to do in Clare'* brochure when the fuse went. Dusk had fallen and, although some natural light remained, he made use of flashlights they had found in the cutlery drawer. His daughter was not impressed but, then again, she hadn't been ever since they arrived. She had complained that the house smelled like her grandmothers laundry basket and felt the place was unusually chilly for the time of year. He couldn't argue about the odour but, personally, he had found the evening to be quite warm if a little heavy and he put her disposition down to the long trek west from Blanchardstown.

The torches were like sabres of light against the growing darkness as they set off in search of the fuse board. He felt that, in keeping with the period of the place, the board was probably somewhere on the first floor so he climbed the stairs leaving Katie to scout around below. He called out regularly to reassure her and she responded in kind. She had exhausted the kitchen and living room when she spotted the door to a broom cupboard under the stairs. She opened it and stared inside. It was dank. She reeled a little from the waft but managed to focus and, as the buckets and brushes came into view, she stepped in closer.

The chill that had toyed with her earlier became more acute now and she felt a distinct breeze that shivered through her uncomfortably. She could hear her father shuffling about upstairs and she offered a running commentary of her find.

"There's a cupboard down here....under the stairs...and it stinks." She scanned with her torch. "I can't see a fuse board but there's a draft coming from somewhere. I wish Mam were here.... she'd know what to do".

Her father's voice had a boom to it as he called out. "Thanks sweetheart. She'll be here tomorrow and I'd appreciate it if you didn't tell her your old man can't fix a breaker when it blows. I thought I'd found it up here but it was a medicine cabinet... moth balls and a bottle of Stewart's Liniment Oil.... holiday home my arse". Downstairs, Katie struggled with the dropping temperature.

She rubbed her arms and noticed the vapour from her breath as it swirled into the torch light. She was more than slightly amused by it.
"There's a winter wonderland going on under this stairs. I expect I'll be found in the morning with icicles hanging from my chin like a white walker. Seriously... you really need to get down here".
She heard heavy footsteps trudge slowly along the upstairs hallway. Their impact caused dust to shower her hair and she shook her head for fear of spiders. She couldn't contain her annoyance. "Jesus, you make enough noise...don't you." The wooden stairs creaked as the footsteps got closer.

She scanned the cupboard one last time and the silence was broken by a faint sound that seemed to emanate from behind the wooden panelling. At first, it was so distant that she was convinced it was nothing more than the night air but then she heard a defined tinkle, a melody; that drew her back in. She leaned forward and listened. The gentle chimes of a music box enchanted her momentarily and she was captivated by it. She did not question it... it was simply sweet and soothing. Then the chimes stopped and the silence was broken by a child's voice that whispered out to her. There was a sadness to it... a longing... as it called out a single name..."Delphine".

Katie staggered backwards so quickly that she banged her skull on the cupboard doorway and she was reeling in pain when the footsteps hit the final step. There was the click of shoe heels on the tiled floor. She called out in pain and her tears flowed silently, inviting the comfort of a fathers love. "I... hurt... my head" and her sobs were pitiful as they trailed off "I wanna go home Dad". But there was a shuffling in the dark and, for the first time, a figure emerged at the edge of her torch light.

There were muddied boots and the shades of an old black suit... tattered at the hems, torn at the seams, a burial robe. Her words were trapped inside her. There was a call of jubilation from upstairs as her father yelled out. "I found it! It was in the back room. Damn thing must be a thousand years old". The figure was upon her now and the ache that stunned her only seconds earlier was now replaced by a numbness that left her blank and hollowed out. There was only silence and vapour as she turned the flashlight on its face. The lights came on just as she screamed and, by the time Jack Markham came rushing into view all that remained of his daughter was a torch that rolled along the empty hall. The police searched for months but to no avail. Even the lake was trawled but no sign of young Katie Markham was ever found.

Her father was a suspect until he became the subject of missing persons investigation himself and neither inquiry ended well. The town was not forgiving of Peter Casey for ignoring its concerns and he lived with his guilt in the only way he knew how. He retired and handed the reins to his son.

The house on Kilchoman Road fell silent again and, perhaps, it should have stayed that way. But the past would have its own voice and it would whisper until someone would listen.

DELPHINE

CHAPTER TWO: WAY BACK WHEN

'They've promised that dreams can come true but forgot to mention that nightmares are dreams too.'
Oscar Wilde – Irish Poet & Playwright

The apartment by Spencer Smith Park was that self-contained, modern living unit that set Canadians back $3,000 a month. It was clean and the space was well utilized but, to Laura Brady, it was little more than a box setting that was grossly overpriced off the plans. The development offered a fitness facility, a laundry, culture hub and suites *'...elegantly designed to the high standard you expect from a Caledonian Condo Complex'* as the glossy brochure had said. Maple View Mall was just down the street with John Brandt Hospital and the bar district a stones throw from there. But she hadn't purchased the property for any of those reasons. She lived in The Sandpiper because it afforded her anonymity and she could come and go without journalists and autograph hunters making an ass of themselves on the grounds. It was a place where she could be alone unless, of course, she chose to have company and she woke this morning to discover she'd made that very choice the previous evening.

He was younger than she was, probably mid 30's and, as he rolled over in the bed and stretched, she recalled him from the Arts & Culture event where he'd been exhibiting several of his works. There had been so much wine or perhaps there hadn't but she'd just made sure to box off more than her fair share. Either way, she'd been drunk and she remembered dancing with him at the afters party. But that was then and this was now and she knew what had to be done. She sat up and shook him until he woke. He looked at her and smiled. She was absolutely black and white. "Get up... C'mon, get up and get out." He seemed confused and he reached out to touch her. She recoiled. "Don't you fucking touch me... now get your shit and get out!"

He went to the bathroom and she heard the shower buzzing as she reached for a Vape on her bedside table. Several clicks later and it came to life. She blew a large cloud as he walked back into the room naked. He was Cuban as she recalled and, as he stood there, he was entirely beautiful in a Havana handsome way. She watched him dress and she walked him to her door. He went to speak but she cut in first. "Don't ever contact me again. Never come to this apartment and never approach me in company... vive una buena vida." He nodded and left.

She sat out by the balcony and watched the traffic speed in all directions like an afternoon ant colony. Car horns blew and buses pulled in front of trucks that crossed paths with vans that edged out cyclists in a never ending battle for dominance and, beyond it all, Lake Ontario sat as just another observer to the chaos. The phone rang and snapped her out of it.

She was wearing a Toronto Toros T Shirt and, as she walked across the living-room, she looked considerably younger than her 50yrs. The call was long distance and the line was poor. The signal strength faded in and out and the volume seemed to vary but she knew who it was from and she identified herself on request. "Yes... yes this is Laura Brady." The caller divulged information that shocked her where she stood.

Burlington, Ontario was as pretty as a picture in the noon day sun. A fresh autumn breeze whipped in by the lake shore but clear skies were bringing out the best in everyone. From his third floor window, publisher Michael Roth could see down Brant Street all the way to the lake shore. There was a festival by the Travelodge and he watched as coaches pulled up and revellers bustled about enjoying the entertainment.

Today was a good day for Roth. Some years earlier he had taken a chance on an untested author and the gamble had paid off. Laura Brady had come to him, back then, as somewhat of a lost soul and he often felt that it was that very quality in her novels that spoke to so many. She appealed to the disconnected and he fully understood that insecurity. More to the point, he knew how to market it.

Her previous novel 'The Last Ship Sailed' had made the best seller's list in more than ten countries and the film rights had been optioned. Now it was time to go again. Laura had wrapped up work on her latest offering, The Olive Grove, in January, having spent the holidays in isolation, and there was very little for her editor to do. Cover illustrations had been approved and today's meeting would focus on a release date and marketing tour. Roth had commissioned a series of promotional posters for Laura's consideration and his table was decorated with images that best captured the essence of the piece and its often enigmatic author. He watched as she pulled into the car park and he noted by his watch that, as always, she was pretty much bang on time.

Laura Brady enjoyed Michael Roth almost as much as he valued her. He had a cynical humour that resonated with her and, when it came to the world in general, he simply wasn't fazed by people's negative opinions. "Opinions are like assholes" he would say "everyone is entitled to their own".

He was good at his job, sharp where it counted and that would make today all the more difficult for her. Their combined sense of drive and determination was a common ground but life was what happened when you were making other plans and fate had rewritten Roth's schedule. He just didn't know it yet. Now it was just a matter of breaking the news and she trusted that he'd be supportive.

Roth sensed her unease from the moment she walked in. Laura wasn't just a writer, she was a collaborator and she was hands on when it came to the process. She seemed distracted and, in a bid to lighten the moment, he asked his secretary for a pot of coffee with two cracked cups. He insisted that one be smeared in lipstick stains and he suggested that the java be infused with several spoons of male chauvinism and just a hint of Betty Boop. He referred to her as 'Toots' and asked if she didn't find the term offensive. She replied that she'd add the conversation to her ongoing harassment case and he agreed that it was probably the way to go.

When the coffees arrived, he apologized and asked his secretary to remember that he made for a better husband than an employer. He asked that she not hold his chauvinistic failings against him when they got home and she said she'd take it under consideration. The exercise had its desired effect and Laura softened but he still sensed the undercurrent. Roth stacked the promo posters neatly and placed them to one side. Business could wait. "Okay" he said "let's get the real issues on the table."

Their friendship had always been an honest one and he suspected that he knew Laura as well as she would want anyone to know. She had always been guarded when it came to her life and he often felt that her avid readers probably identified more about her through her novels than those who knew her personally. He regarded their relationship differently however and there was an openness between them that usually dispensed with caution. Saying that, she led into it tentatively and he could see she was struggling.

"You know my history... I mean when I was a child... you know what happened?"

DELPHINE

He poured the coffee and slid a cup her way. "Well... I know you were adopted... if that's what you're talking about". She had been avoiding his eyes but now she drifted to them. "That's not strictly true. I was never formally adopted... I was farmed out to family here in Canada. Somewhere along the way, in some corner of Ireland, a 'mother'... and I use the word carefully... found herself in a situation where the best option available to her was to hand her child to folks who would take her thousands of miles away. I was 2yrs old for Christs sake".

Roth was familiar with the story and just restated his view. "You say it was the best option available to her.... but maybe it was the only option, you don't know that." Laura was quick to reply. "Yes and that's the problem. I don't know. I never have. If she'd found herself with a newborn that she simply couldn't care for, then I'd understand. But she had me for two whole years and you'd grow to love a dog in less time". She sat into a leather armchair and leaned back. She closed her eyes tightly before continuing. "And another thing, if she wanted rid of me, then why the gifts? Every year... and I mean every single fucking year... a gift arrived on my birthday, no card... no note, just an acknowledgment that I still existed for her... that I was still real." Her hair sheltered her face but her despair laid jaded on her features.

Roth was patient, as always. He nodded as she spoke and there was a certainty in his voice when he responded. "I think you could be wrong about that. I think it was her way of telling you that she still existed... that she was still real." He sipped his coffee and continued. "It must have come as a helluva shock to you when you heard from the nursing home."

She gathered her thoughts and sighed deeply. "I didn't even know there was a St Gabriel until I got the call. I discovered my mother through an admissions slip, a goddam admissions slip of all things. 'Next of Kin... Laura Brady'. They had my contact details and an instruction that I was never to be contacted. Never. No matter what. Imagine that."

She raised her eyebrows and tried imagining it herself. "I think it was her way of closing the loop before she checked out. But, of course, the medical expenses needed to be paid and that's how I learned that my Jane Doe finally had a name.... Eileen Brady." She stood and browsed through the promo posters.

Roth jumped on the opportunity. "Jane Doe.... now there's a great title for a novel... just saying." Sensing her disapproval, he apologized sincerely and continued. "What amazes me is that the family who raised you never spoke of her. I mean... you must have had questions."

She sighed deeply and he saw that those questions had eaten more than their fill over time. Her voice was flat. "Hey, they were good people... just not my people. They did their best but I was always on the outside, at least in my mind I was." She did not want Roth's pity and her voice picked up.
"Oh they tried... they surely did... and they gave me many good things growing up but nothing they ever gave me could compensate for the one thing they refused me... answers... and that was not just what I wanted, it's what I

needed. " She became upset and the mask finally slipped. "I got a call from St Gabriel's early this morning. Michael... she's dying."

He tried to console her but there was such raw emotion in her words that he felt he was simply going through the paces. She stared through him as she continued. "She's dying and I have to go there. I've spent ten years writing novels that get to the truth and I'm damned if I don't live my own life that way." Roth was unequivocal in his support and the business of business was less than secondary right now. "Of course. You must go. But I wouldn't be a friend if I didn't state the obvious." He was measured in his words and spoke them slowly. "There's a reason... Laura... why you've never gotten those answers. Now, I don't know what that reason is... and neither do you... but maybe, just maybe, you're better off not knowing." She gathered her things and turned to him. "I leave for Shannon tonight. I'll take a hire car to Drumasheen." She stared through Roth in a way that sat uneasy with him. "Who knows, maybe she'll be gone by the time I touch down but, when you look in the mirror Michael and wonder who you are, then and only then will you understand the silence that stares back." She promised to keep in touch and she left. He stood by the window and watched her drive all the way down Brant Street, where the festivities had suddenly lost their colour.

The Irish weather was decidedly indecisive. In the hours after dawn, the sun had committed itself to a hard days graft but, shortly after breakfast, it rolled under a blanket of clouds and thought better of it. The rain came down as no more than a light drizzle but it spattered across the dry earth causing the mists to swirl ankle deep. Laura hadn't driven a stick-shift in many moons and the gears of her airport rental bellowed angrily as she chugged her way along Kilchoman Road. To add to her woes, and probably her embarrassment, a herd of sheep were being moved between fields and she found herself surrounded by them. A red faced farmer tipped his hat to her as he gathered them up and he cleared a path for her to follow. She could still hear them bleating as she rounded the bend but their voices faded surprisingly quickly as the house came into view for the first time.

It looked utterly abandoned. Ivy had found its way along the façade and it had wrapped itself around the corners like a ragged napery. The windows were coated in a fine dust and the entrance door stood as a stained symbol to Victorian grandeur. The branches of a twisted oak reached out from an overgrown garden but, as she got closer, Laura was pleasantly surprised to come upon a young girl, perhaps 4yrs old, skipping happily just beyond the tree. She noticed Laura, smiled and continued as though she wasn't there. Laura called out to her. Once again, she smiled in response but nothing more. Laura felt that the child was notably old world in appearance and, quaint as it was, it seemed decades out of place. Her hair, unnaturally curled, was set off by red bows that matched the frills and sash of her ruffle terraced dress. Even the skipping rope, with its faded bobbin handles and knotted twine, seemed out of period.

As Laura approached, she was startled by the creak of the entrance door as it crept open. She could see the pitch black darkness of the hallway inside and there was the faintest outline of a broad staircase but it was vague at best. The silence was broken by the cries of a new-born emanating from deep within the house. The skipping rope hit the earth for the last time and its owner discarded the toy in the long grass. She stared at the ground in silence and Laura felt that there was a moment where time seemed frozen. She felt the chill for the first time and it shivered right through her and the new-borns cries grew louder and more distressed. She raised a hand in farewell as her lips began to tremble.

The bow haired girl looked to Laura but this time her face was drowned in sorrow and her eyes were pools of despair. She slowly raised a hand in goodbye as her lips began to tremble and Laura felt that she was fighting back a river of tears. As she neared the door, Laura became aware of a figure hidden in the darkness. It was tall and the trickle of light that seeped into the hallway allowed her to identify the extremities of a gaunt feature or two. The child turned back to face Laura and there was a striking sense of resignation to her that was matched only by her fear. Her eyes left Laura's and she stared out across the fields. She focused on something in the distance, a point well beyond the property, before slowly stepping inside where the darkness swallowed her up and the door closed. The cries of the new-born became muffled but they continued. Laura had wanted to call out but her words were trapped somewhere deep in her chest. She could feel a desperation crawl up along her back but there was a powerlessness that hobbled her. She heard a latch being lifted and turned to see a gate swing open in an adjoining field. The farmer and his flock made their way forward without as much as a single sound. As Laura watched them, her attention was attracted by something in the distance. Further down the field, two figures stood motionless.

One was taller than the other with the smaller figure almost childlike in stature. Both were draped from head to toe in what appeared to Laura as loose black sheets. The morning mist danced about them and there was nothing between them but a silence that was both surreal and short lived. The cries of a new-born breached the stillness and the sound of its weeping resonated from all directions. It cut through Laura and she covered her ears as she winced.

The flock huddled together and they stared blankly as they became aware of the figures. The cries grew louder and a terrible fear consumed them. They turned in unison and ran at full sprint. They launched themselves, in panic, at the perimeter walls and they screamed out to Laura, their eyes upon her as if begging for mercy... pleading for refuge. The noise was deafening and as Laura reeled backwards, she saw the figures move, slowly at first but then they lurched forward at pace. They were gliding swiftly when Laura found the energy to flee. She turned and ran but, in doing so, she tripped herself up and staggered straight into the outstretched arms of 'The Widow Woman' who's mourning shawl enveloped her...and the crying stopped.

Laura woke with a start and found an air hostess hovering about her in concern. The flight was mid Atlantic, she imagined, and the lights were dimmed as passengers caught some shut eye before touching down. The hostess explained that she had been quite animated in her sleep and that she had no option but to wake her. She offered Laura a beverage and they settled on a Chilean red. As she sipped, Laura could still detect a tremble in both hands and she had to lean forward to meet the glass halfway. The nightmare may have been over but Roth's parting words echoed inside her. She wondered if that foreboding hadn't played some part in the desperation of her dreams. She felt that the stress that surrounded this trip was taking its toll on her. She certainly hoped it was just that.

CHAPTER THREE: DELPHINE

'Death is not the greatest loss in life. The greatest loss is what dies inside us while we live.'
Norman Cousins – US Political Journalist & Author.

The Burren Arms was that boutique style hotel that would gladly welcome travellers if Drumasheen had any to boast of. It was well maintained and quite inviting but, other than the occasional fishing party or jolly boys outing, it could never be regarded as busy. The bar was popular with locals on weekends and the carvery lunch brought a respectable day time trade but the hotel had never lived up to the potential that Shane Kelly had hoped for when he bought the place some years earlier.

He had invested and advertised, even launched a local music festival on the hopes of attracting outside custom but he learned the hard way that Drumasheen could be cruel to those who embraced change. Local weddings went a long way to paying the bills but breaking even was a goal that he rarely achieved. Furthermore, rural Ireland was not always accepting of same sex relationships and, although they took his femininity in a light-hearted if sometimes lewd way, two middle aged men holding hands outside the chipper was a bridge too far for the Padre Pio brigade. When his partner wilted under such pressure and moved on, Kelly put The Burren back on the market but it came as no surprise when the estate agents went quiet.

DELPHINE

Like everyone else in the town, he had simply learned to live with his lot and his loneliness.

Today would be a special day for the hotel however and Kelly hovered about the lobby in his best suit and brogues. Laura Brady, bestselling author and occasional scriptwriter, would be taking up residence at The Burren for a short stay and there had been a buzz about the place since the booking was confirmed. But, to him, this meant so much more. He was an avid fan and her characters had been a friend to him when the world and its despots closed their doors. He could identify with them, he understood their pain and her novels occupied a very special place in his life. He would not share them so he had travelled to the bookstore in Ennis and bought copies of her last four titles which were now on display at the reception counter. He had offered to have a car collect her at Shannon but she opted for an airport rental as she said she had some things to attend to. He stood on the hotel steps like nervous groom and waited on her arrival.

When Laura eventually pulled up, she was not at all what Kelly had expected. He had imagined that her success would have infected her with that wicked air of celebrity but she was not at all outstanding in that sense. Although she had recently turned fifty, he could have been excused for suggesting she was much younger and, as she stood by the car in faded denims and distressed leather, she looked more
Cripple Creek than Rodeo Drive. He introduced himself and took her suitcases inside. The books at reception amused her somewhat and he sensed a slight

embarrassment when he asked her if she'd sign them. When Laura asked who she should sign them for, he felt his own embarrassment and said "Ah...if you could sign them 'To Shane'...they're actually for me."

Like all small town traders, Kelly was inquisitive and he was curious as to why Laura would find herself in a lost backwater like Drumasheen. He made it clear that they were delighted to have her at The Burren, of course, but he wondered what the locality had to offer beyond good food and cold beer. The question made her a little uncomfortable, not that it was intrusive but that she didn't fully understand how to respond. He was making his apologies when she cut across him. "I have family here...at least I think so. I suppose you could say I'm searching for my roots."

Kelly was amused. "Well, if its roots you're after, we can start with mine." and he leaned forward so she saw his greying hair do its best to overcome the cheap bargain basement dye. Laura found him funny and she was certainly warming to him. He asked if she had a starting point for her search, a name he might help her with. `It surprised her that she felt so nervous in mentioning Eileen and Roth's words of warning echoed yet again as she spoke. "I'm looking for an Eileen Brady." she said softly "I understand she's in a retirement home called St Gabriel's."

Her sense of nervousness was greatly heightened when she saw the expression on Kelly's face. His cheeks faded pale at the name. He stared at Laura in silence and when he spoke, the levity was lost from his voice. "You

don't want to go out there." he said and he shuffled uneasily "You'd be best off to avoid it." Laura was confused. "Out where... St Gabriel's?"
Kelly was whispering as staff busied themselves about the lobby. "No... That house. It's old and... It's... unsafe." Laura was more bewildered than ever. She pushed him on the matter "I'm sorry Mr Kelly, I don't understand...what house?"

He held her hand in both of his and his concern took her by surprise. He paused for a moment and sighed so very deeply before continuing. "I found myself alone of late but your stories... your heroines... they embraced me when no one else would...and I feel indebted to you for that." She felt an overwhelming sadness exude from him but there was also a raw honesty. "So I beseech you, please avoid the place and hope that it avoids you. Jim Casey will know best how to handle such matters when..." he stopped and felt suddenly awkward but he finished. "when Eileen finally leaves us."

Rather than clarify matters, he had only succeeded in compounding her confusion and he could see that an apprehension had gripped her. She spoke in a whisper. "Jim Casey?" Kelly was edging away as he replied. "Jim's the solicitor. You'll meet him tomorrow. Now... we have a wedding party in and I'll have to take my leave." He disappeared behind the reception desk and she carried her own luggage to the elevator.

That night was difficult. Perhaps it was the change of scenery or the circumstances or simply the jet lag but sleep came to her only in pockets and each time she woke, she could feel an icy chill that defied even a double duvet. The bar had stayed busy long after closing time and the faint tones of traditional Irish music could be heard until 2am. She had gotten up shortly after that and went to use the bathroom. On the way back, she noticed that her closet door was opened and, on latching it shut, she caught her reflection on its full length mirror. She looked lost and she certainly felt it. She tossed and turned for another hour before finally drifting off but it was a troubled slumber and her dreams were unkind. She woke shortly after 9am and was pleased to find a dry but slightly overcast morning gawping through her windows. It was welcome even if the day itself was not. Laura would travel to the nursing home in search of answers and, as she lay in bed for a few final moments, she wondered if Roth had a point about the dangers of digging. Some boxes are best left closed... or were they? She headed for the shower not at all noticing that the closet door lay fully open again.

Drumasheen was a West of Ireland market down that afforded farmers and traders the opportunity to sell produce and animals to the local community. As she drove slowly through the village, she felt that the streets were a curious blend of nostalgic charm and base neglect. Shop fronts that would not look out of place on a postcard rubbed shoulders with derelict buildings crudely boarded up and around them she noted a late 19th century architecture that stood chipped and sparsely painted as if the town itself stopped caring sometime in the roaring twenties. The great depression might have started on Wall Street but, as desperation was biting from the Big Apple, she felt something just as devastating was sucking the life blood from the veins of Drumasheen. She followed the sign posts and, soon enough, she was pulling into the car park of St Gabriel's Nursing Home. The case nurse was most understanding. She knew who Laura was but deliberately focused only on the patient, Eileen Brady. She gave Laura a brief history as noted in the file. Eileen had lived a great many years in the family home, a large country house set not too far off the Kilchoman Road outside the town. She had lived there alone following the passing of her mother and it was highlighted in the file that Eileen had given birth to a child, a daughter, in the 1960's but no further details were stated. Her mind had slipped over time and she began to live in a world fabricated by her own nightmares. By the time that the staff at Gabriel's came to take her, she was demented by her phantoms and she had lived a truly terrified existence inside those walls. When asked of her dependents or next of kin, she had submitted a notebook with Laura's details, addresses over the years, phone numbers, work history prior to publishing, writing history after publishing and some newspaper clippings relating to interviews. The nurse said that Eileen had been largely silent since her arrival a few years earlier but she was often heard whispering as if in deep conversation and they found her hiding on a few occasions when she was first admitted. More recently, she had lapsed in and out of comas and, sensing that Eileen was into her final stages, they had made the decision to reach out to Laura so that, at the very least, there would be family at her funeral.

Eileen's room was more homely than one might expect. Though she maintained a distance in her final years, she had tended to her surroundings and one could imagine that she had sought solace there. Pressed flowers filled a variety of frames about the walls and the lampshades were charmingly old world as was the leather armchair by the bed. But the curtains that adorned the double window seemed decidedly out of place or, more specifically, out of time. They were flamboyant in colour, an absolute pallet of balloon reds, sky blues and daffodil yellows, and depicted images of a carnival or a circus, far more suitable for a child of the '50's than a 21st century senior citizen. This seemed rather odd to Laura but it was a triviality. The moment was finally upon her and, after waiting so many years, she neared the bed with surprising trepidation.

Eileen looked as though she had just passed away peacefully. Her hair had been brushed off her face and her cheeks had been dusted with a rouge that complimented the frills of her cream silk night gown. She looked so frail and so very tiny that Laura wondered if she should touch her at all but instinct being what it is, she leaned in without thinking and kissed the old ladies cheek. She traced the contours of her face and followed each line and wrinkle. She held her hand and watched as the veins formed tapestries beneath the thinning skin. She wondered how

DELPHINE

different they might have been the last time she held them and she kissed them gently.

Laura sat into the armchair and watched over Eileen until sleep took both of them.

When she woke, it was late afternoon and the effects of the flight were still slowing her thought process ever so slightly. She sat up and looked about the room to establish her bearings. She saw a bottle of spring water on the other side of Eileen's bed so she walked quietly and poured a glass. As she drank, she noticed a single greeting card that read *'Goodbye, I'm really going to miss you'* on the front. Laura wondered what kind of person would give a farewell card to someone so close to death. She opened the card and saw a simple message in ink *'M waits by the carousel. Candy floss a penny. Kiss her for me'* and it was signed *'K'*. Laura looked back to the curtains and noticed the carousels hidden among the dancing giraffes and the tuba playing elephants. As she placed the card back, Eileen let out a groan and shifted slightly in the bed.

Laura had really hoped the old lady might wake but she was still out and the movement seemed nothing more than a reaction to discomfort. Laura leaned in one more time and whispered "Miss Eileen... it's me... Laura. I've come back to be with you." There is a desperation in her voice. "I have so many questions... and I can forgive. Jesus Christ... I need to forgive." She was startled when Eileen's eyes slowly opened and her tears streamed into her hairline. She was staring past Laura, at a point on the ceiling and her voice was barely above a whimper as she spoke. "So... sorry..." Her voice trailed off but the tears kept coming. Laura was telling her to rest when she spoke again. "So... sorry... you came back." Her eyes locked onto Laura's and her voice strengthened a little. "You were saved. Your mother... loved you." A panic sets in and she grabbed Laura's hand. "Go back... he knows you're here now. You were... saved... saved! How could you come back?" A terrible pain shot through her and she arched her back before screaming out "Marie... Marie I'm so sorry sweetheart." The staff nurse came running in and, between them, they managed to settle Eileen down. Once they had, she drifted off again leaving Laura dazed and confused.

It was evening by the time Laura returned to the hotel and winters night had descended. The lobby was quiet but music drifted from the bar and the wedding party appeared to be in full swing. She stood by the archway leading to the open pub and stared inside. Revellers tapped toes as musicians beat out a rhythm that had customers sway and beer pumps pour in unison. Shane Kelly was working the crowd and she watched as he darted from table to table laughing with one group or frowning with another, weaving with each dynamic as the mood called for. Several burly men, who chugged stout and balanced their bellies on overworked leather belts, waited for Kelly to pass before one leaned forward and pinched his buttocks. The proprietor looked offended but yielded to the guffaws of the mob and accepted it. He stared past them to the archway and, upon seeing her, his face lit up with the sincerity of an honest smile. He beckoned her to join him and he pointed to a fiddle player as if she might know him. She did not and she respectfully declined his invitation. Instead she shuffled to the elevator and went to her room.

It had been a long day and she felt several thousand miles from home. The problem, as she saw it, was that she could say the very same thing if she was sitting in own living room back in Burlington. She was disconnected and, often as she tried, she could never really remember a time when she wasn't. The family who raised her had done their best but, regardless of the circumstances, she was somewhat of an imposition and she knew that from the early days. Kids can be cruel and, with her flaming red hair and her face full of freckles, they never allowed her to forget the Irish that was in her so she rolled with the punches and so did they. But there was a need in her that could not be satisfied and she sampled all the vices as the years passed by, from drink and drugs to prayer and sexual partners, all to excess and all to no avail. She felt fulfilled only in the world of fiction and in the pursuit of justice for her characters.

Reality was never easy and today had drained her absolutely. She had hoped for one moment of clarity, anything at all to fill that void, but she had more questions and less answers and it wasn't supposed to happen this way. As the music drifted up from the bar, she envied those who danced and clapped and were drunk with laughter. They were together and, as a cheer went up from the crowd, she recalled doing shots alone and lines alone and feeling alone with every lover she ever laid down with. She needed to belong and she needed to experience the release of something other than a blade on her flesh. She peeled back a wristband and thumbed a jagged scar beneath without glancing at it. Whether she was drunk or drugged or just plain fucked, the sensation never filled the need but it took the focus off it for a time. It was simply escapism and the less she knew about her bedfellows, the better. She did not undress. Instead she curled up and waited for sleep to take her.

The call came through shortly after 9.30am and Laura was awoken to another grey morning at her window. When she answered, a polite receptionist informed her that Jim Casey was waiting in the lobby and that he had ordered coffees for two. Laura got up but felt an icy chill in the room. She put it down to the fact that she had slept as she did and headed for the bathroom. She was stopped by the open door of her wardrobe. She distinctly remembered locking it shut and she did so again. It locked firm but she wondered how or why it unlatched so often. It was not such a concern as a curiosity and it drew a smile from her. She hit the shower in more positive mood.

Jim Casey sat in the lobby of The Burren Arms and thumbed through a fresh copy of The Parting Glass by Laura Brady. The cover depicted an eye shedding crystal tears but the artist had developed the blue/green tint of the iris into a vague representation of the globe. He was not necessarily an art lover but the richness of colour and the contrast of shade had captured his attention. The elevator opened and he watched as Laura stepped into the foyer. He stood and held the book aloft to catch her eye and it worked. She studied him carefully as she approached. He was probably early 50's, of average height, a little soft around the mid-rift but he sported a black/grey striped blazer over a white grandfather shirt and faded jeans so that he looked decidedly out of place in the legal profession as she knew it. She also recognized him as the fiddle player from the bar and she now understood why Kelly had pointed him out. He began by apologizing that his voice was slightly hoarse and said that the party had gone on much later than expected. He poured her a coffee and she noted that he was shaking off the effects of a hangover. This surprised her.

"So... you're an attorney?" she asked.

He emptied his cup in one swallow before he answered. "Christ no miss, I'm just a small town solicitor. A Rolex watch and a reputation away from an attorney." He looked directly at her, sighed and smiled. "There's a wedding party in town and I was drafted in as a session musician for the past few nights... drunk as God intended."

She was still observing him as he poured another java. There was an air of incredulity in her voice as she spoke. "I thought the wedding wasn't until today". He found great humour in the comment and he enjoyed her naivety. "You've obviously never been part of an Irish wedding. The party could last all the way to the divorce. Mine did. Anyway... welcome to the wilds of West Clare."

He reached out his hand and she shook it without replying. Breakfast consisted of eggs, sausages, bacon and a black pudding that she simply couldn't countenance. He relished it and, when the plate was almost empty, he buttered freshly baked soda bread and scraped it across the remnants to soak them up. They talked. She told him about the visit to Gabriel's and he explained that Eileen had lost her mind many years earlier. He said that his father had been solicitor to the Brady family before him and that he had inherited the family in a sense and that he would answer her questions if he had the answers. He went on to say that layers of secrecy shrouded the family over the decades and that, over time, rumour had replaced fact on many things.

It was vague at best. Laura took it in and raised the issue of the house. "Of course they had to have lived somewhere but a family home wasn't something I ever thought about." She finished her coffee. "Perhaps it's something you can tell me about at some point." He placed a twenty beside the bill and stood up. "No time like the present. It's a fifteen minute drive and I have the keys." He stands and stretches so that he reaches to heaven. "It's just a little remote so, if it's all the one to you, I'll drive."

If the village of Drumasheen had seen better days, then the surrounding countryside suffered a neglect that was both bleak and beautiful in equal measures. As they drove. Laura imagined that the summer might have been kinder to the community but, with winter bearing down and storm clouds often looming over the horizon, it was hardly the stuff of postcards. Several miles from town, they turned off from a tarmacadam road and weaved between the rain filled potholes of a bog road. On the far side of a wide bend, they encountered a red faced farmer moving a herd of sheep between fields and the car was momentarily surrounded by them. Laura was gripped by a sense of deja vu and, when the farmer smiled in the window and tipped his hat as he had done in her dream, she felt an anxiety crawling about her like an infestation. The roof arch of the farmhouse appeared in the distance and its gable end windows stared blankly like eyes that were grieving. They pulled up next to a gnarled old oak tree that stood guard by the front of the house and Laura was first to get out. The house was exactly as she'd seen it and she stared beyond the tree half expecting to see a little girl lost in time. But they were alone and that eased her somewhat. She glanced out across the fields and found only the wind waltzing with the winter barley. Jim had been fumbling through a set of keys and had located the one he required. He glanced up as he spoke. "Pretty bleak eh? Daylight doesn't lend itself to this place. Just means you can see the cracks with more clarity." He noticed a concern in her. "You okay?" A gull squawked on its way elsewhere and she traced it until it disappeared over the farmhouse roof. When she replied, her voice was barely discernible. "I've dreamed of this place".

Jim found this amusing. "Jesus...you're easily pleased. If I had your money, I'd be dreaming of a villa in Santorini and something with a soft top but that's just me." He took on a more serious tone. "For what it's worth, this place will be yours very shortly. Eileen's had a long life... a troubled one as it goes but she's destined for a better place... if you believe in that kind of thing." The conversation continued as they walked toward the

Edwardian porch. She found him to be acceptably cynical. "You're not big on positivity" She told him "I sure hope you generate more joy with a fiddle under your chin." She scanned the house again. "I meant I saw this place in a nightmare. They must run in the family." He held up the key for further identification and spoke as he inspected. "Houses like this turn up in every kids nightmare. Perhaps you read the newspaper articles and they stayed in your mind." He had walked several feet ahead before he realized she had stopped and he turned to face her confusion. "What newspaper articles?" He was quick to explain "My apologies, I forget that you didn't grow up here. It was such a story... I just thought it might have made the Paddy papers over there." Her patience was running low and her agitation was evident. "Do I have to speak in single syllables until the liquor wears off? What... news... paper... articles... James?" He cuts through the apologies and his reply is stark. "A girl disappeared here. Just a kid really. She was with her father and, according to him, she simply vanished in a black out." He noted the horror on her face but continued anyway. "There's a lake at the back of the house and it was trawled but nothing was ever found. Suspicion went on the father, of course, but long after the investigation ground down, he came here many times to search for her." His voice weakened. "What happened next was just as tragic."

Dec 2012: The image of a full moon shimmered on the calm lake surface as a single row boat bobbed gently in its glow. Bo Chen Yang secured his fishing rod and dropped a line as Pavarotti serenaded from a battery operated radio that perched at the bow of the boat. Bo put a flame to a packed Churchwardens pipe and the first clouds of smoke rolled upward. He sat back and enjoyed the moment. At times like these, he would often remember spending evenings with his father on Lake Namtso back in their Nagqu Prefecture but that was many years ago and China hadn't been home to him in over three decades. He stroked his greying beard and fixed his woollen hat over his ears. Suddenly the line snagged and his reel started spinning out of control. He grabbed the rod and began a tiring battle. He yanked one way but the great weight pulled against him so he took the line in both hands and started reeling it in manually. Whatever it was, it was nothing he'd ever encountered before and he strained under the stress until, eventually, he could feel something yield and come toward the surface. He leaned in as he hauled the line and the outline of some huge creature began to emerge from the dark depths. One more tug and his bounty became clear. The badly decomposed body of a man broke the surface and rolled over to reveal a bloated aberration snagged at the shirt collar by a fish hook. As Bo watched, the cadavers' mouth slipped open at an askew angle and a crab shuffled into view. Bo reeled backward sending Pavarotti to the depths and the corpse disappeared back into the murky darkness.

Laura was truly horrified. "It was the young girl's father." Jim informed her. "Divers fished him out the following morning but Bo was never the same after the incident. He still gets a little crazy sometimes if you ask me."

She thought about and asked the obvious. "And the girl... nothing?" He shook his head slowly and he was genuinely grim. "No... nothing... this town has a past and she was swallowed up by it...just like the others." He attempted to walk away but she reached out to halt him. "Others?"

Jim sifted through the key ring and selected one. "I'm sure you have better places to be today so I suggest we get on with the tour." He turned the lock on the great wooden door and its hinges screamed out as they creaked open for the first time in many years. Even this early in the day, the hallway was dark as net curtains draped on a kitchen window obscured the light coming through. A staircase rose up along the right side of the hallway with a kitchen entrance to the end and a drawing room to the right as they entered. As they walked from room to room, Laura was struck by the volume of religious iconography on display. Crosses hung from every wall and Sacred Heart pictures sat beside weeping images of the Madonna and Child. Jim Casey drifted upstairs as Laura wandered along the hallway. She ran her fingers along the panelling beneath the stairs and was surprised to detect a cold breeze blowing from a clear crack down one length. On inspection, she discovered that the crack was cleanly angled so that it was, in fact, a doorway that someone had attempted to paper over in the past. She was about to tear at the strips when Jim Casey called out from above and she went to join him. Jim had opened a closet in one of the bedrooms and a large hatbox could be clearly seen tucked into the top shelf. He pointed this out and she asked if he could retrieve it. He did and they placed the box on a dusty double bed that sat in the middle on a dusty dour room where they removed the quaint, old lid and stared inside. There were photos, all aged, some faded, that captured moments long since passed and Jim gently spread a selection out for better clarity. As they sifted through them, Laura became focused on a single picture of a young girl, perhaps 3-4yrs old, who was standing to the front of the house holding a skipping rope with bobbin handles. She had a bow in her hair and she looked notably forlorn. Behind her, the great wooden door is opened and Laura can make out a vague outline in the dark of the hallway. She ran her fingertips along the outline and, as she did, a melody suddenly chimes out from the top shelf of the closet. Casey had to hoist Laura up at the knees but she reached deep into the shelf and removed a vintage music box that was still opened and chiming sweetly as she removed it. The box itself was remarkably unremarkable with the dark wood exterior sparsely decorated in gold leaf along the edges. The interior was lined with a rich red satin and there were trinket drawers that lined up snugly but it was the ballerina that caught Laura's eye. She was porcelain perfection as she raised one pump to knee level and her arms arched upward as she pirouetted to the sweet chimes of Elgar's 'Salut d'Amour'.

   Laura was enchanted by her and, before Jim can break the moment, she whispered the name 'Delphine' Jim had intended saying something quite different but he found this more interesting. He was curious and it wasn't often he found himself with that emotion in Drumasheen. He looked to Laura. "Delphine?" he asked. She didn't take her eyes from the box. "Yes...it's what they called her." He looked at the box and back to Laura. "And how would you know that...exactly?" She closed the box and the melody was cut short. She stared beyond it to nothing in particular. "I don't know. I just do." She turned to him and there was such a confusion in her voice. "Jim...who opened it?"

He was browsing through the photos again. "The box? Well I suspect it's been open like that for years. Most probably wound too tightly and became unstuck as we moved about. I get like that myself sometimes." He looked around before continuing. "I can't imagine anything other than memories has blown through these rooms in over ten years." He waved away a cloud of dust that spiralled as they gathered the photos back into the hatbox. Laura placed the music box on the window ledge and they went down stairs.

As they left, Laura asked Jim for a copy of the house key. She said she might like to visit from time to time. He stopped by his car and stared at her so intently that it slightly unnerved her. Noticing her anguish, his intensity lightened and he smiled but only a little. "Of course. The house is as good as yours anyway."

She looked back one more time and, unaware of the grave consequences, she asked a question that would change everything that she ever knew to be true or believed to be real. It was the question Roth most feared. "My story... will you tell me where it starts?" He took a deep breath and sighed. "It starts with Edward and

DELPHINE

Anna...and The Great War." They sat into the car and he started the engine. He spoke again before they left. "Let's talk over the coming days and I'll explain what I know." He sought her approval and she nodded. He reversed and they turned onto the bog road.

The rooms of the house fell dark and silent once more. Shards of light broke through and captured the dust the swirled in the aftermath of such a rare visit. The music box sat on the window ledge and faced out to the world. The silence was broken by a shudder that ran through the very fabric of the house. It was a wave that cut through the walls and the rooms and through time itself. It peeled a century of age from the corners and the cracks and the glory of a home once loved was restored in all its warmth and colour.

A woman's voice called out from downstairs. "Edward, the photographer will be here soon. Don't be so tardy." A young man, early twenties, emerged from an upstairs room. He was tall and handsome if ever so slightly gaunt. He was adjusting the braces of his impressively creased trousers so that they fit over the shoulders of his collarless shirt. He stopped and ran his palms on either side of his slick centre hair parting before disappearing down the stairs.

CHAPTER FOUR: ON FLANDERS FIELD

'In the bleak midwinter
Frosty wind made moan
Earth stood hard as iron
Water like a stone
Snow had fallen
Snow on snow on snow
In the bleak midwinter
Long, long a go'
Gustav Holst / Robert W Smith

July 1914: Although events in central Europe were casting a long shadow over government buildings in London, Paris and Berlin, talk of conflict was kept to a minimum in the townlands surrounding Drumasheen and people went about their business oblivious to it. The marriage of Edward Brady to Anna Cussen had been a great affair and the wedding would be talked about for some time.

It was a union of two fine families and the Cussens were more than happy to accept young Edward as his father had passed away only a year before and he had found himself without kinship. In turn, the Brady home had been bequeathed to him and the Cussens stood proud in the knowledge that Anna had married well and would be well cared for. She stood at the bottom of the stairs and watched Edward fumbling with his braces as he skipped off the last step. She was quick to address it and she fixed the braces in place so that his jacket fit neatly and he looked every inch the fresh faced groom. He leaned in and whispered. "Anna, you're a gem. What did I do to deserve a wife like you?" She was wearing a white dress with a ribbon to the side and her hair was up so her youthful beauty was unhindered. She replied as she fussed with her hair pins. "You don't need a wife, you need a mother. Just as well I can be both." There was a knock on the door and she sprang into action. "That'll be the photographer. I heard he has a Kodak camera from New York City so he's probably charged us half a crown just to knock on our door." She got Edward outside and finally fixed her hair pins. He hugged her gently to reassure her and spoke with such honest affection. "Well... you're worth it. I always want to remember you as you look right now" He stood back and smiled "You're beautiful." She blushed and brushed past him but she took him at his word and she felt like she'd stepped straight off a Renoir.

The photographer was a quirky little man with spectacles and a waxed moustache. He busied about his tripod until all was ready and he raised a hand to indicate he was happy with the pose. He called out from beneath his camera hood. "A smile from the newlyweds." They stood perfectly still as he snapped and the moment was captured forever. It was a moment of such significance as it was, in some ways, the last moment of the life they had known and that life would be stolen from them in the moments that followed. As the photographer gathered his equipment, there was a commotion in the distance and they walked to the roadside to find out more. A young man from the village was running toward them at speed and he was calling out. He was badly out of breath as he reached them and Anna addressed him. "Good Lord, what's all this about? Such a commotion."

The young man took several deep breaths and blurted out the news. "Wars broken out... in Europe. Mr Asquith is sending troops to fight the Kaiser and some of the men in the village are wanting to enlist. I'm taking the news to the farms." He ran off down the old Kilchoman Road and disappeared around a bend, still shouting. The photographer grabbed his tripod and camera and set off on his bicycle toward the larger commotion in the village. Anna and Edward were left alone to contemplate the news. They walked slowly toward the house and she saw that he was visibly shaken. There was a tremble in his voice. "My God... war." Anna was quick to quell his fears. "This is not our war. If Asquith wants to take the Germans to task, then so be it, but it means little to our community." She stood in front of him and stared through him. "It means little to us."

He was avoiding her eyes as he answered. "If it spreads, it will mean something to all of us... whether we like it or not." He looked to her and there was a raw honesty in his words. "Father didn't leave very much when he passed and the Kings shilling is worth as much to me as it is to any man."

A panic rushed through her and she could feel him slipping away even as he stood there. "No. Never! Your place is with me and we won't discuss this again." Even though her strength was on show, her tears could not be contained. She cupped his face in her hands. "We'll manage... together." He smiled and extended his arm for her to link. "Walk with me by the lake." She rested her head on his shoulder and they sauntered past the gable end of the house as the sun was swallowed up by angry clouds.

St Gabriel's was busier than usual. Nurses and visitors whipped by with wheelchairs while the old and infirmed leaned on walkers as they ambled at their own pace. Laura walked up the main hallway flanked by a doctor on one side and the staff nurse on the other. They entered Eileen's room and Laura was taken by the sight of a fresh bouquet of flowers that brightened it up. The colours were radiant and the fragrance was sweet as it filled the air. The doctor was outlining their position. "I'm afraid that Eileen is beyond our treatment now. Her heart is strong but I suspect she will not wake again and our focus now is only to ensure that her passing will be as painless as possible." Laura appreciated the effort and took the opportunity to offer her gratitude. "I really can't thank you enough for everything. You've been wonderful." She took a lungful of the flowers. "The bouquet is stunning. Your staff didn't have to do that."

The staff nurse interjected and informed her that the flowers didn't come from them. "They were left here by the lady who came this morning. She didn't stay long and she was old, so we assumed she was a friend." She gave a curios look before continuing "It was the oddest thing. She wore a bonnet with a veil. I haven't seen one of those in such a long time." Laura attempted to quiz her further but the doctor assured her they had rounds to do and they left.

By the time Laura returned to the hotel, night had fallen and she was exhausted. Perhaps the jet-lag hadn't fully worn off but she found herself drained as each day passed and, no matter how early she bedded down, she was simply jaded from noon onward. She looked inside the bar and, in the midst of the crowd, she could make out Jim Casey bopping to the rhythm of a Ceili session. She felt such a strong urge to join them but she needed sleep. She was almost at the lift when a pretty young receptionist called out. Laura turned to acknowledge her but stayed by the lifts. The receptionist held up a package wrapped in brown paper and clear cellotape. She informed Laura that it had arrived earlier and that it felt as though it contained a book of some kind. Laura remembered that Roth was to send a copy of 'The Olive Grove' once the covers had been agreed so she told the receptionist that she'd collect it in the morning and she headed to her room.

Sleep came quickly and she drifted into its very depths. A dog passed on the street and barked out in search of company as the last cars of the night cast their beams across her ceiling and were gone. The latch of her closet door turned slowly and the panel swung open in absolute silence. The temperature dropped by several degrees and Laura's breathing became a vapour but she remained unfazed. A tall, gaunt image appeared from the closet and cut a ragged outline as it approached her. There was a wheeze to its breath that rasped with each exhale and it loomed over her from the base of her bed. It opened its mouth and the cries of a new-born infant broke the silence. It screamed out in a fearful desperation and it yearned for pity.

Laura woke with a start to find her window ajar and she rubbed her arms against the cold wind that whistled in. She locked it secure and looked about the room. The closet door was closed shut and nothing appeared out of place. She climbed back under her duvet and drifted away.

September 1914: Anna Brady paced across a sparsely furnished room and stared out the window. The avenue was empty so she paced back to a fireplace packed with burning logs and turf. A matching sofa and armchair occupied the centre of the room and a gramophone was mounted on a wooden stand with a collection of neatly packed records stacked beside it. The door opened and Edward walked in. He was in full military uniform and he was carrying a leather luggage bag. He stood proudly but his voice was lost in sadness. "Well... how do I look?" The moment overcame her and she burst into tears. He embraced her but there were no words to ease their pain.

He sifted through the records and placed one on the gramophone. He pushed the sofa aside and, as the first strains of 'After the Ball is Over' filled the room, he took her in his arms and they waltzed in silence. The flames flickered as they floated by and, for the briefest moment, the world was beyond them. Then three knocks broke the moment and they just held each other as the song faded out. Three more knocks came and they shuffled to the hallway and opened the door to the porch. An Officer of The Royal Munster Fusiliers stepped forward. He respected the moment and nodded to Anna. "Corporal Vance ma'am, Spectemur Agendo, Let us be judged by our Acts. The Fusiliers will see him right." He turned to Edward. "It's time to go son."

Edward collected his luggage but, as he stepped forward, the Corporal took a camera and asked them to pose one last time. Anna was devastated as she stared into the lens and Edward did his best to look stoic but he was broken hearted and it showed. He kissed her softly but his lips trembled as he whispered that he loved her. Vance told Anna the photo would be sent to her and, as she stood on the porch, she watched as they climbed into the back of a British Army truck. It trundled away down the avenue and she could see Edwards face as he stared back from the throng of young men also off to war.

The weather had picked up and sunlight filled the lobby as Laura waited for the day receptionist to sign out some guests. Once they had gone, she approached the counter and asked after the package that had been delivered the previous day. When it was handed to her, it was not what she'd expected and it threw her completely. The package was crudely assembled and the name Laura Brady was scrawled across the front in blue ink. She turned it over and found nothing. She determined that it

DELPHINE

contained more than one item and this was certainly not from Roth. There wasn't even an address on it.

She asked the receptionist if she knew anything about it and the young lady was pleased to inform Laura that she'd actually taken the package in the previous day. "I'm sorry" she said "It was quiet busy with the wedding party when she came to the counter and simply asked that you get it. She was gone before I could ask any questions." Laura was totally lost. "Who was this woman? Do you know her?" The receptionist had no clue who the woman was but did say that she was old and she wore a bonnet with a lace veil like a throwback to another time.

Laura sat at her bedside table and unwrapped the package. It contained a series of handwritten letters, a ledger and some photos in a clear plastic pouch. She opened the pouch and carefully removed the pictures. There are five in total. The first had faded with time but it was clear enough to show a young couple from a bygone age. He was tall and handsome, dressed in a collarless shirt and trousers with braces under a fashionable jacket. His hair was slicked black and parted perfectly in the middle. He was young, perhaps 20, lean if not ever so slightly gaunt. She was younger, 18 at most. She was wearing a white, full length dress with a ribbon at the waist and her hair was neatly tied up. They were both smiling. Laura turned the photo. On the back, in faded ink, was written *'Edward and Anna 1914'*.

The next photo depicted the same young couple but, this time, he was in full army uniform. He stared out from under the peak of his cap as she stood by his side. Time had taken the definition from their faces but nothing could hide their sadness. They looked so utterly crushed and Laura thumbed the contours of their faces in some sense of sympathy. On the back it read *'Edward. Off to war. 1914'.*

The third photo brought an instinctive gasp of concern from Laura. It was taken several years after the others. They stood by a fireside in what appeared to be the drawing-room of the Brady house. He was slumped into a chair. There was a vacant look about him. His head was tilted to one side and his hair was unkempt. He was staring blankly at nothing in particular. There was a blanket pulled up around him and he looked so terribly frail. She was standing behind him with her hand on his shoulder. Even though the photo is old, the weariness was there for all to see. There were no smiles. On the back it read *'Edward and Anna 1923'* Laura was unnerved by the next image. This photo showed an older Edward. He was standing in the open doorway of the house. He was dressed in a black suit with a waistcoat. His eyes were sunken back but there was an intensity about them. They were filled with the disconnection of death itself and that was truly unsettling. Two young girls sat on the front steps with an opened music box between them. One was shying away from the camera lens. The other was defiant of it. On the back it read *'Eileen and Kathleen 1939'.* The last picture was a Polaroid and it was in colour. It showed two women, early 40's, sitting on a sofa in the drawing-room of the Brady house. On the floor, two children aged perhaps 2 or 3 were playing with a music box. No one is smiling. On the back it read *'Eileen and Kathleen with Laura and Marie 1970'*. Laura was stunned. Though more than 40yrs had passed, she could still identify Eileen in the photo. She stared at the children. She stared at herself. The phone rang and she was startled back to the moment. She answered and immediately regretted it.

Eileen laid peacefully in the bed with her hands folded on her chest. Laura was crying as the duty nurse tried to console her. The doctor spoke with respect "I'm so sorry Miss Brady. But it may help to know that she passed away quietly. Death comes to us all and we can only hope that it's a gentle guest. In Eileen's case, it was a welcomed one. She is at rest now." Laura was struggling through her tears when she thanked him and the staff for all the support they had given and she asked if she might be afforded a little time with
Eileen alone to say her own goodbyes.

It was proving harder than she had anticipated when she first touched down at Shannon. Losing Eileen wasn't just the loss of family but, with her passing, Eileen would take so many secrets to the grave and Laura had no one left to fill in the gaps. She sat by the bed and held Eileen's hand. The room was quiet and she whispered her last words in the silence. "You're at peace now... finally. I wish I could have known you ... that we could have known each other." She stood and leant across Eileen. "I wish I knew about them all... Anna... Edward... Kathleen...

Marie. Farewell and safe journey." She kissed Eileen gently on the forehead and the moment was rocked when she felt the fingers lock onto her shoulder. She pulled back to find Eileen's clouded eyes open and fixated upon her. The old lady rose up and, as Laura staggered backward, Eileen's eyes blindly followed. She slipped and hit the ground with a heavy thud. Eileen's voice was guttural "He's... found you... Laura. Only Bigali... can save you now. Stay away... from that house." Laura began scrambling to her feet but lost her footing in the panic and she fell backwards again. Eileen stared ahead and started humming the melody from the music box. Laura screamed out as Eileen slowly laid down and folded her hands over her chest. Her eyes closed and she was, once again, at peace. The medical team rushed in and found Laura huddled in a ball.

December 25th 1914: Anna Brady sat beside a turf fire and stared into the flames. The gramophone was playing Handel's Messiah and she rested as the shadows danced about the fire hearth. As the last strains of the oratorio faded out, she allowed the silence to fill the rooms of their home and she walked along the hallways, running her fingertips along the walls as if she would find some news of him there. She waltzed alone into the kitchen where she found an unopened bottle of red wine. She picked up a mug and drifted back to the fireside. She opened the bottle and watched the flames through the stream of Merlot. Even though it was early in the day, she drank from the mug and it eased her just a little.

Edward Brady held a tin cup to his mouth and shivered throughout as snow fell heavily all about him. He was draped in a long coat with a balaclava about his head but the French temperatures had plummeted on the northern front and the trenches were hard as iron for the British and Belgian troops pitched deep within them. Across no man's land, the Germans were camped in equally cruel conditions but the middle ground laid free from the pounding of shells and the rallies of rifle fire that were the trademarks of battle. Word had filtered through the troops that Pope Benedict XV had called for a Christmas ceasefire and, although it had been officially rejected, death facing up from the pits was enough motivation for the foot soldiers to lay down arms albeit momentarily. The snow, however, had not agreed a thing and it fell till it numbed their flesh and burned their features.

The silence was broken by a sound that surprised everyone. It was a young private, Edgar Alpin, who sang out the first nervous lyrics of 'In the Bleak Midwinter'. His voice carried and it brought grown men to total silence as it drifted out across no man's land. Edward leaned back and lent his voice, singing out in support and one by one they waded in until it was a choir that sang with their hearts and their souls. As the last words went out, each man was lost in his own memory and someone back home was loved without ever knowing it. The silence was broken again but this time it came from the German side and an older, richer baritone voice sent out the powerful strains of 'O come All Ye Faithful' with all sides joining in. When the singing ended, a German voice called out "No shoot... no shoot!!" and the first ragged men appeared from the trenches and staggered across the bleak open space between the sides. They began gathering their dead as the allied troops appeared and lent their assistance. Edward searched through the bodies for a familiar face and found the lifeless body of Corporal Vance who had collected him that first day in Drumasheen. As he brought the bloody remains to a safer burial hole, Edward locked eyes on a German soldier attempting to do the same for his fallen comrade. They stood facing each other and offered a mutual blessing that they might both make it home when this was all over. As they did, the sound of a distant plane brought them, once again, to silence and the sound of faraway shelling sent them back to their frozen pits.

Jim Casey was waiting for Laura when she returned from St Gabriel's. She was badly shaken as he approached her. He sounded rushed but concerned. "I got a call from the hospital. They told me what happened. Jesus you must be exhausted. Are you okay?" She walked straight passed him on her way to the lift. She was seriously pissed. "For someone who's just been assaulted by a corpse, I think I'm doing pretty damn good." She stepped through the doors onto the lift as spoke directly to him. "I have something to show you and I want the truth do you hear me? No more bullshit."

DELPHINE

Once they were in her room, she handed him the photos and poured two stiff drinks as he sifted through them. She handed him a whiskey and her voice had a composure to it when she spoke. "I need you to tell me what you know about these people... please." He looked to the photos and looked back to her. There was a reluctance in him and she could see it. She spoke again and there was a quiver on her voice. "Please." He picked the photo from 1939 where the much older Edward is dressed in his black suit with waistcoat. Jim stared for a long time and found that the past still unnerved him. He spoke in grave tones. "Edward Brady... my father was terrified of him. Scared the shit out of me a few times I can tell you. All the kids were spooked by him... sitting out front watching us like we were dinner. He was your grandfather. Anna was his wife, your grandmother. There were stories about him..." He finished his whiskey and went for another but she stopped him. She wanted clarity. She demanded it and he wasn't going to dilute the truth with firewater. She stood over him and tapped her toe anxiously. "The stories Jim..." He sat up and assumed a doubting Thomas approach. "Well, you've got to remember it was a time when people were deeply superstitious." She'd had enough and she blew. "Oh Jesus Christ enough of this!! Hoodoo or not, I need to know and you need to tell me. Now...the stories!!" He sat awkwardly and moved uncomfortably but he finally peeled back the veil. "It was said that... something happened to him during the Great War. A story circulated... that he had encountered something... a presence... in the mountains of Turkey... some even said it was Satan himself. Jesus, I feel so stupid even saying it." Laura felt a sudden pain shoot through her shoulder and she pulled her top away to reveal black bruises where Eileen had grabbed her. She massaged the damage and continued. "Where did the stories come from?" Jim picked up the photo of the young Edward and Anna from 1914 and he handed it to her. She scanned the image and looked up. "Anna?"

He nodded and stood up. "Afraid so. She claimed that the parish priest told her... a Father Tiernan I believe. I think she probably lost her marbles." She was rather dismissive and more than a little annoyed. "There's a lot of crazy people attached to that house.

Eileen, Anna... Bo Yang the Chinese fisherman. Don't you find that strange at all?" He shrugged his shoulders as he sifted through the photos. "It can happen in small towns." Her annoyance turned to frustration and she blew up again. "Oh for Christ's sake stop! You might think I'm losing it too but I know what I saw today and there's nothing normal about any of this." She calmed a little and took a slow deep breath. "What about the others?" She picked up the photo from 1970 and scrutinized it closely. "Who is Kathleen... and who's Marie. Eileen kept saying her name over and over and, now that she's gone, you're probably the closest thing to a living relative I have in this God forsaken place." He took the photo from her and stared at it.

DELPHINE

He took his time before answering. "Actually...that's not true. Kathleen Brady is your aunt... Eileen's sister. She tried to burn the house down shortly after that photo was taken. She went a little..." Laura cut across. "Crazy...I know. Where is she now?"

He put the photo down and sat back. "She lives outside the town. Not too far from the family home as it goes. She's rarely seen around here and I doubt many would even remember who she was." He changed the subject. "This may not be a priority to you right now but have you eaten?" She appreciated the gesture and gave a faint smile. "Ever or just today?" He smiled in return. "Let's start with today. I know a decent place a drive away from here." She got her coat and they left.

December 1914: Madame Butterfly wobbled ever so slightly on the gramophone turntable and the Aria 'Un bel di vedremo' reached out to every corner of the house. Anna Brady ran down the hallway and pulled the front door open. The town postman was standing outside fumbling with a sack satchel looped over his shoulder. He seemed startled by the intensity of Anna's excitement but he reached into his mailbag and produced a well packed envelope with an air mail postmark. She beamed with delight and went inside. The aria was nearing its crescendo as Anna sat by the fire and opened the seal without tearing it. She held it to her nose and closed her eyes as she searched for any scent of him. She removed the letter and settled back. She read aloud. "My dearest Anna, today is my birthday." The separation overcame her and she held the letter to her lips. She continued reading in silence as the music drifted throughout the empty rooms.

The day was bright and clear. They'd driven to a tavern in a small fishing village by the sea and Laura was sitting outside when Jim appeared with a waiter carrying hot soup and lattes. Laura looked about and the setting appealed to her. She took a lungful of sea air and let the sun embrace her face. The weather had been kind to them and the gentle breeze that washed over them was fresh but soothing. The sea lapped against the harbour and recently painted boats bobbed on the waves. But the serenity was not what she came for and she moved quickly back to the conversation. She placed the photos on the table.c"You were telling me about Kathleen."

He ran his palms over his face as if tiredness was taking over again. "She was institutionalized after the fire... gone for some years. When she was released she used to dress in mourning clothes, bonnet and veil included. Eventually... she just faded away."

Laura looked at the photos again and stared at the faces of the children. "And Marie?" He sipped his coffee and his tone is deeply sombre. "To the best of my knowledge, she was your cousin... Kathleen's child. There was a tragedy. She was playing by the lake and she fell in. You were sent to live with family in Canada shortly after that." He thought for a moment and his words were well considered. "The family never really mixed with the towns people... and the towns people certainly didn't mix with them... they avoided the Kilchoman Road like the plague."

The waiter approached the table and asked if they needed anything. They smiled but declined. Jim stirred his soup slowly and tapped his spoon several times on the side of the bowl. He took a deep breath and stared directly at her. "You and Marie were a mystery. I don't think a single person in this town even knew you existed. But my father visited Anna before she died... she was rambling by then... but she said some things that he recalled... all very vague I'm afraid."

All agitation was gone from her voice and she was calmer. "What became of them in the end...Anna and Edward?" He looked to the heavens as he thought. "Let's see... Anna passed away in...'72 I think it was." She looked back to the photo and her voice trailed off as she asked the next question. "And Edward?" He spoke quite deliberately. "Edward passed a year before her. The church wouldn't allow him on consecrated ground... so he's buried out by the lake." A look of confusion crossed her face. "Why would the church refuse him a Catholic burial?" He shrugged his shoulders. "I don't exactly know what happened. Maybe you'd be best off talking with Kathleen but, I warn you Laura, she really is unstable." She shook her head as he said it and asked one more question. "Before we go... have you ever heard the name Bigali?" He thought for a second but the name meant nothing and they decided to take the conversation elsewhere.

The tavern was getting busy and a tour bus had pulled in. Several dozen retired Americans disembarked.

They smiled to the locals who welcomed them openly. Laura was rather taken by this. "This is nice. Reminds me of the lake-shore in Burlington." Jim stirred his latte and bit into his complimentary biscuit. He was just happy that the conversation had changed but he had wanted an opportunity to learn more of who she was and he figured this was as good a time as any. "Is that where you live?" Steam rose from her soup and she sipped on her coffee while she waited for it to cool. "Yes. Burlington, Ontario. 747 Brant Street... like the plane, you know." He stopped chewing as the joke sank in and he chuckled quietly when it did. "You like it there?" She gave the question its due respect. "I've lived in worse places... lots of them. I moved to Burlington a few years back. I'd moved around a lot before then... a bit of a restless soul." They watched as a trawler pulled into the bay and several oil skinned men came onshore. One of the men noticed the couple sitting outside the tavern and he approached. Jim became unhappy. "Shit... it's Bo Yang. Just smile and let me do the talking. He's a nice guy but he can go on a bit." Bo Chen Yang came close but kept a distance of several feet.

    He wore a woolly hat and sported a light grey beard. He eyed them and smiled but his curiosity seemed focused more on Laura. He smiled and nodded as he spoke. "Hello Jim... hello lady. Strange to see you so far from the town. I would shake your hand but..." He extended his hands to present soiled palms. "...the sea has its stench." Wiping his palms along the front of his oilskins, he dug into his pocket and produced a ready packed pipe. Jim was formal but not entirely friendly and he addressed Bo as he brought the pipe to life. "Bo, this is Laura Brady, the writer. She's in Drumasheen for a few days." Bo looked at Laura and his smile carried a genuine warmth that she felt immediately. He blew a cloud and spoke through it. "I know who you are. My wife, she loves your books. You are here because of Miss Brady in St Gabriel's. She was always such a good woman. I hope she will recover." Laura broke the news with a gentleness and she could see that Eileen's passing had truly affected him. He removed his woolly hat in respect.

Bo blessed himself and kissed a cross that hung from a silver chain round his neck. "Death is... a terrible thing." He bowed his head and his voice was distant. "My deepest condolences." Jim had intended bidding Bo a good day on the hope that he would leave but Laura got in first. "Speaking of death, Jim told me that you were the one who found the body in Brady Lake." Jim reacted angrily and protested that the incident was irrelevant but Bo was not fazed by the subject. He put his hat back on and fixed it in place. He spoke calmly and without hesitation. "It's okay Jim... not a problem." He smiled and stared directly at Casey as he continued. "I will tell the truth of that story to anyone who will believe me. You may think I'm crazy but I know what happened." Laura looks from Bo to Jim and back. "Jim thinks the whole town is nuts Bo. I'm only here a few days and he's already marked me down as bat shit crazy. I was told that you were fishing when you discovered the body." Bo stared at Jim but spoke to Laura. "Is that all he told you?" Casey wanted no more of it and there was a rage in his voice when he sat forward and barked out. "Bo... enough!! Let it go... both of you... I implore you... let... it... go!" But Laura would not be outdone and the secrecy would stop here and now. She had lived under that veil all her life and she hadn't travelled all this way for more of the same. She spoke to Jim first "I want to hear this. I need to hear it!" Then she turned to Bo. "What really happened that night? Bo composed himself before continuing.

      Bo Chen Yang was struggling with the line. Using both hands, he slowly drew the object closer to the surface. He could see the shape appear from the murky pool as he pulled with all his might. The body broke the surface and rolled over so it is staring skyward; a crab crawled from the open mouth which startled Bo but he composed himself. He reached out to haul the corpse in when the water broke again and another face appeared by the side of the dead man's head. It rose out of the lake so that only its sunken eyes were above the water line and they stared at him in a hellish mix of decomposition and wrath. Yang was frozen in place. He wanted to scream but the sound was trapped deep in the pits of his lungs and his pipe dropped from his mouth with a plop and disappeared beneath the black waters. There was a surreal moment of absolute silence when they locked eyes before a ravaged arm rose up and grabbed the corpse, pulling it back down to the dark depths. The creature maintained its glare until it vanished, with its booty, beneath the waves. Bo Chen Yang scrambled back in the boat knocking the radio overboard. He grabbed at his oars and began rowing frantically, screaming aloud in the quiet night as he headed for shore.

Bo still looked disturbed. There was a faraway look about him that took some moments to pass. He was drawn back slowly but his words were clear. "There is a terrible evil out there Miss Brady. I had heard you were at the house and I just thought I should tell you what exists there." He adjusted his hat and stepped back. "I will leave you good people to your soup. It lacks a little pepper here I find. Anyway, good day to you both and my heartfelt sympathies for your loss." He bowed his head and clicked his heels to attention before wandering off through the tourists who buzzed about. Laura watched as he went to join the other fisherman and they begin unloading lobster pots. She stared at her crab soup as Jim sat in silence and slowly shook his head. She took a moment to gather her thoughts. "I think I've lost my appetite. Could you take me back to the hotel? I have letters to read." Bo stopped his duties and tracked the vehicle until it disappeared around a bend. He took his cross and kissed it again before grabbing a lobster pot and getting back to work.

Laura sat in a lobby armchair as the hotel staff milled about. She was tired, not for the want of sleep but for the absolute need of tranquillity. She stared outside and found that dusk was still some way off. She walked out onto the hotel steps and took a lungful of western air. It was cold and had the very faintest hint of Christmas. Most of all, it had a calming effect and she responded by exhaling until her lungs were spent. She sat into her car and started the engine. The road ahead was an interesting alternative to the byways and bohereens she'd already travelled. It ran through vast patches of rural land and she could see farmhouses dotted along the hillsides that rose up on both sides. Up ahead, she could see forest trees and she was greatly heartened to find that the road cut a path directly through them. Sycamores towered in from left and right and their branches leaned in to form a canopy above her. Her car radio honed in to a local radio station just in time to catch the opening strains of 'At Seventeen' by Janis Ian. Laura opened both passenger and driver windows so that the cool evening air flowed through and her hair danced about in sympathy to Janice Ian's sad but familiar tale. She sang aloud as the daylight began to fade.

It happened so suddenly that Laura had to brace tightly in her seat. It was a blur but something scurried from the woodland and under the wheels of her rental. She could feel the crunch as she ran over it and she slammed on the breaks so that the car swerved around and her lights highlighted a small, broken body on the arch of the road. She rested her head against the steering wheel and gasped for air. She looked up on the hope that the creature was gone but, alas, it was not to be and an overwhelming sense of guilt gripped her as she slowly climbed from the vehicle. She walked back along the road and, upon nearing the spot, she discovered that the animal was a rabbit or, at least, it had been. Blood had sprayed liberally and the creature was badly broken but she could see its tail and ears and it genuinely hurt her that she had ended such a simple life. She knelt down beside it and mourned its passing. Its eyes stared ahead but the blood had leaked from the mouth and nostrils. Laura wondered where it was going to at the moment of impact and she imagined a youngling that might need feeding or a partner waiting in the undergrowth. She was devastated. She was getting up as if to leave when the rabbit squealed out and its body began to writhe in agony. Laura was caught completely unaware and the image of something so innocent in such pain was almost too much for her. The animals' innards were displayed on the road but still it fought on. Laura looked through her tears and saw a hand sized rock nearby. She reached out and picked it up. Although crushed inside, the creature was still moving and she could see it staring across the three feet of road that separated it from it from the freedom of the tall grass. It was a journey the animal would never complete and Laura knew what she had to do. As she raised the rock in the air, the rabbit appeared to accept the gravity of the moment. It froze in fear and she could see its chest rise and fall with great rapidity. She paused for just a second and, as she did, the creature cried out one more time. But this was not just the squeal of a broken beast. For her it was the passing of innocence, the pain of abandonment and she wilted completely as the tears became a river that she had no control over. She brought the rock crashing down on the rabbit's head but its entire body spasmed and it squealed out for mercy. Laura brought the rock down again and again until, finally, there was a silence in the winter dusk and she climbed to her feet. She tossed the rock into the undergrowth and, shortly after, the car drove carefully over the remains and disappeared in the direction of Drumasheen.

DELPHINE

CHAPTER FIVE: BACK TO THE FRONT

'I don't live in darkness, darkness lives in me'
Dr Seuss -US Author

The wedding party was finally over and guests had left throughout the morning. By mid-afternoon, the lobby was running at normal pace with just the cleaners busying from one area to another. Shane Kelly lent a hand where he could but he didn't want to miss his opportunity so he kept one eye on the door and the other on the matters at hand. Laura arrived into the coffee dock shortly after 7pm and night was settling in well by then. She had recently freshened up but she still looked so very tired and, with Eileen's passing, he wondered if he shouldn't approach her at all but it got the better of him and crossed her path. "Good evening Miss Brady. May I take this opportunity to extend my condolences. I heard the news." She sensed his honesty and ran a palm gently down the sleeve of his jacket in affection. "I thought we had a deal that you call me Laura." She closed her eyes and, for a moment, she allowed her ordeals get the better of her. "It's been a really crazy day. I'm miles away.... or, at least... I wish I was miles away.... but there's simply no place to run... not really" She could see his awkwardness and apologized. He instinctively embraced her and, after a moments hesitation, she embraced him fondly in return. His face was so filled with hurt and when he spoke, she could hear that pain. "Losing someone you love, even if it's to the world and not just to death...it's like dropping from a high wire and falling so far that you never know when you'll land." He seemed more lost than she was. She noticed a novel sticking out from a jacket pocket and she was familiar with the sleeve. "The Night Before Dawn... wow, that brings me back." She smiled and raised her eyebrows "Not my biggest seller as I recall." He produced the book and held it with both hands and with great reverence, almost as an offering. "I just love this book. Your heroine, she was... so blissfully broken." He thumbed the cover. "I understood her like she was a sister and I often wondered how much of her was in you... or you in her." Laura smiled and nodded slowly. She took the book from him, produced a pen from her shoulder bag and wrote an inscription just inside the cover. She closed it and handed it back. She kissed him lightly on the cheek and walked toward the elevator. He opened the cover and read *'To Shane, my brother in the Burren. Love always, your eternal sister, Laura.'* She turned in time to see him press the book to his lips as tears trailed down both cheeks.

The shower was hotter than normal but she wanted it that way. She rested against the wall and let the water cascade over her as the images of the day flipped past by like a nickelodeon. Was it real... Eileen? How could it be? But she saw it and she had the bruises. Faced with death, had she simply fallen over and come down on that shoulder? But she remembered everything in such detail and, as she stepped from the shower and faced the mirror, she saw the separation of fingers in those marks.

She dried herself and donned a bathrobe. She went to the bedroom, poured a Baileys and took a deep blast from a Vape that she'd left on the bedside table. She sat in her single armchair and rested. The Vape blew plumes into the air and she sent a trio of rings spiralling through them. She sipped her whiskey cream and her eyes were drawn to the package and its contents.

She scanned through the letters and, for the first time, noticed that they were numbered 1-5 at the back. She decided to follow them by the numbers and she opened the first and it read:

'Occupied Territories Ottoman Empire,
August 15th 1914
My Dearest Anna,
We have been stationed in a camp on the Dardanelles hillsides above Bigali. Last week, the Aussie boys arrived and they've settled in well. In the evenings they sing billabong songs and we trade our tobacco for their whiskey.'

Edward stood by the edge of the camp and stared back in. He was in full uniform with a brown leather utility belt strapped across his tunic. He was carving out the figurine of a waltzing couple from a rough block of wood as a group of soldiers at the centre of the camp sang Waltzing Matilda by a burning fire. All seemed well and his eyes are drawn beyond them to the staff tents which were clean and sturdy given the circumstances. He turned his back to them and looked to the mountains. There, in the dark and dotted along the ridges, he caught fleeting glimpses of Turkish villagers as they brandished burning torches and remained almost entirely still. They watched the camp with great interest and he watched them with great concern.

> *'The locals are wary of us and they keep their distance. We have noticed them in the evenings guarding a pass that leads deeper in to the mountain. I think they may have moved some of the old folk to a safe location there as the Ottoman and Serbian troops have been cruel at times.'*

The snow had fallen for several hours and the temperature plummeted. Edward sat with the troops and they were silent as the sound of shelling got louder in the distance. The men got weary and unwashed. They stared from one to the other in sombre contemplation as the shelling got closer.

> *'I miss you terribly and I countdown the hours until we are once again together. When I get home, we will put this war behind us and spread our wings in a safer world'*

The troops were on foot but the ground was wet and slipped from under them; the terrain was uneven and the road was nothing more than a muddy path for donkeys and livestock. The men marched in silence as the air was sub-zero and it was often too thin to endure. As they plodded forward, there was a melody that caught the entire platoon off guard. A young Turkish girl, perhaps 8 or 9 years of age, sat at the fringe of the path and watched the men pass by. She had on her lap a wooden orchestrina, a music box that tinkled a sweet tune and they listened as they sank into their own thoughts. A single soldier broke hurriedly from his ranks and knelt by her. It was Edward.

He opened his supply bag and removed a loaf of bread along with two tins of canned meats. He offered them in exchange for the music box but the child was conflicted and shook her head rather shyly. Her eyes lit up, however, when she saw the carved figurines in his satchel. He held it up and, with its in depth detail and varnished finish, the couple looked quite splendid. He placed the piece with the supplies. She eventually smiled and the trade was done. Edward whispered something in her ear and joined the others once more, he allowed the box to play as they trudged back to camp. Before they turned a corner on the road, Edward glanced back and saw the girl standing with a man who might have been her father. He was holding the carving and, if Edward wasn't mistaken, he was weeping openly. He caught Edwards's eye and waved him off.

> *'For a single moment I was but a kiss away from you. I will keep it as a symbol of our love and of all that is good and sweet. The reis a ballerina that pirouettes and I have named her Delphine after the*

DELPHINE

Parisian dancer. I will be with you in my dreams my wonderful Anna.

Your loving husband Edward'

A boiled kettle switched itself off as steam gushed from its spout and swirled about. Laura emptied a latte into a mug and did a 50/50 with the boiling water and the Baileys. It was hot and hit the back of her throat. It would do just fine. She sat back down and scanned the letter briefly before placing it back in its envelope and opening the next one. She read:

'Occupied Territories Ottoman Empire,
November 7th 1915
My Dearest Anna,
Today is my birthday. Francis Dargan from Enniskillen appeared into our billet this morning with a cake he'd picked up in the village. He's such a character. Perhaps you will get to meet him on our return.'

The soldiers ate cake off tin plates and the mood was joyous. They clapped Edward on the back and there was honest laughter. A sergeant entered and the laughter stopped abruptly. He beckoned them outside and they followed in total silence. They huddled about the sergeant and he spoke to them in hushed tones. Occasionally he glanced to the mountains where the Turkish villagers were on guard. The soldiers stood to attention as the sergeant called for volunteers. Edward was one of twenty who stepped forward. The men started gathering supplies.

> *'Some of the officers are concerned that the locals are storing guns and shells for the Ottoman troops on - route to the front. They feel we should send a sortie up there to see what's going on. I volunteered to go.*
>
> *I'm certain they are simply protecting the aged but I really need to get away from here. It is so terribly cold and I fear we will perish if we do not move. The shells seem closer each night and I suspect the call may come soon. You are my only love. I was a fool to come here. This is nobody's war and these are just people waiting to get back to their lives as you and I are. I will write again soon.*
>
> *Your loving husband*
Edward'

Laura folded the letter carefully and placed it back in the envelope. She took the photo of Edward in uniform and surveyed it as she sipped her coffee. He looked so young and innocent. She picked up the next envelope and found it was bulkier than the others. She opened it and removed several pages. She read:

DELPHINE

'Occupied Territories Ottoman Empire.
November 15th 1915
My Dearest Anna,

A great tragedy has befallen us. Several days ago, we set off to breach the mountain pass. We encountered protests along the way and we were cautioned to return to our camp. There seemed to be a dreadful fear among the locals. They are a simple and superstitious people who believe they have contained something diabolical . . . an Iblis . . . in a fortification on the frozen caps of the mountain. They called this place 'Şeytanın Beşiği' The Devil's Exile.'

The icy conditions hampered the troupe as they edged forward along the mountain path. They were dressed in heavy duty winter coats with gloves and woolly hats that were pulled down over their ears but their breathing was laboured. They carried their Browning rifles at the ready stopping now and then to rest as the terrain became ever more unstable in the fading sunlight. As the trail cut steeper into the mountain side, the men were startled to encounter villagers who appeared from the dark in clusters and implored the troupe to turn back. Some fell to their knees and offered up round blue amulets that they called Nazars. Others raised their hands to heaven and cried out to Allah.

The soldiers would not be deterred however and they ploughed forward regardless believing now, more than ever, that the villagers were offering sanctuary to some enemy or other.

As they emerged from the pass, they witnessed something that brought the entire troupe to a halt. There was a fortress ahead, an entrance into the mountain that was fortified by wooden strips draped in Nazars and other religious relics. Armed villagers lined the entrance and they held burning torches that illuminated their panicked faces. As Edward and the others got closer, the villagers raised their weapons and pleaded with the soldiers to leave.

An older man shouts out to them. "Lütfen bırakın ... Allah adına bırakın lütfen. (Please leave...in the name of God please leave.)" There was panic on both sides now and the soldiers raised their rifles nervously. Both sides took a stand and, in the unbearable tension; a weapon was accidentally discharged. There was a fire fight and gun blasts lit up the night like firecrackers. Several villagers were killed and the survivors absconded.

Once the area was secured, the soldiers began pulling down the barricade at the entrance to the fortress. The officers constructed burning torches from rags and strips of the wooden fencing.

Once inside the entrance, they carefully descended a concrete stairwell to a single chamber where they found a stone altar topped by a huge coffin, a sarcophagus perhaps 9ft long, strapped in link chains with locks. An ornate wooden cross laid on top of it.

DELPHINE

The cross was removed and the locks were busted. They prized open the heavy coffin lid to reveal in the flickering torchlight a thick black mass.

The icy winds whipped about the chamber and no one uttered a word. The company sergeant tested the coffins curious contents with the barrel of his gun and the silence was broken when the mass exploded into a million black flies that burst forward, sending the panicked men scrambling to the floor. The foul swarm ascended from the pit and disappeared through the fortress entrance and became lost into the dark night.

The remains in the coffin were quiet remarkable; they were terribly decomposed but, as the men held their torches closer, they witnessed something that stunned them back to silence. The cadaver appeared contorted as if it had perished in great agony.

Its appearance was almost human but far too large for any man and its hands were curled in claw-like grips. They brought a torch toward the head and the men recoiled in horror. The face was utterly demonic. The lips had been eaten back to reveal teeth more akin to those of some carnivorous beast. The creature snarled at them in death.

Around its neck, there were two gold chains, each clasped to an amulet. One soldier reached in and plucked one free. He held it up and to see the core of the amulet contained a rich red viscous substance that glowed in the torch light. Suddenly there was a great commotion outside and the officers rushed to the fortress entrance. All along the mountainside, swarms of flies were attacking locals who had stayed in prayer. The company sergeant turned to his men and exclaimed in horror, "Sweet Jesus...what have we done?" The men looked to each other but no one found an answer.

Laura held the letter closer to the light as night had well and truly fallen. She was absolutely engrossed but also deeply affected as she read:

> *'On returning to the camp, we found that the swarm had beaten us down the mountain and a shocking insanity had taken hold of our camp. The men were entirely deranged. Our sergeant ordered us to stay back for fear of contamination and we stayed nearer the pass. That night we did not concentrate on the shells of Gallipoli. The screams from the towns people as our own troops butchered them will haunt me forever. We said decades of the rosary as the carnage raged. I have made a pact with Francis Dargan that we will report the atrocity on our return to civilization. I can write no longer as my tears weigh me down. I just want to go home and, if life gives me no more than that, then I will have been blessed by God.*
>
> *Your loving husband Edward'*

Again, Laura folded the letter with respect and slipped it back into its envelope. She placed it back on the table and looked to the others. There were two letters left but the handwriting on the front of one differed from all the others. Only one was from Edward. She opened that one first. It was only a few lines long. She read:

'Occupied Territories,
Ottoman Empire,
December 3rd 1915

> *My Dearest Anna,*
> *Our orders have come through. We are going to the front. Should anything happen to me, I have asked Francis to bring my belongings home, in particular the music box, for it has given me such peace in this wicked place that I do believe my soul would rest easy in it. Should I not return, its melody shall be my voice to you in the long days ahead? I have been and always will be yours my sweet lady.*
> *Your loving husband,*
> *Edward'*

Laura took the photo of the happy young couple and placed it in the envelope with the letter. She sighed deeply and reluctantly reached for the last letter but the phone rang and she was distracted. It was Michael Roth and his voice was greatly welcomed by her. "Hey... I just wanted to pass on my condolences. Rachel was in contact with the nursing home and we're both so sorry. How's it been there?" That was a question she had pondered herself and she wondered if she would begin with the resurrection of Eileen or the massacre at the mouth of hell so she decided to say little until she knew more. She fingered through the letters and held up the last one. She inspected the envelope. The writing was entirely different from the others. She took a hit from her Vape as she spoke. "It's been...interesting." Roth was respectful of the situation. "I just wanted to check in on you... make sure you were okay. So... you getting the answers you'd hoped for?"

She put the letter back on the table and stared at it. "I don't know...maybe." He felt he was encroaching on her time so he got through the business of business as quickly as he could. "Try to relax over there. You've got a busy schedule waiting for you. The Social and CityLine have you booked and Dan over at HBO wants to do something big. Phones been ringing all week... but I have it covered." He waited for her reply but she was miles away in more ways than one. He understood her silence. "I'll let you get back to it... stay in contact Kiddo." She appreciated his commitment and she apologized for being absent. They said goodnight and she ran a shower.

The room was in darkness and the clock on the bedside locker had a red display that pulsated to a rhythm. It read 3.25am every other second until 3.26am was more appropriate. Laura was plunged into the very deepest of sleeps and she laid motionless beneath the heavy double duvet.

The silence was broken by a latch turning and a hinge slowly creaked open. Laura's breath turned immediately cold and a vapour was visible on each deep breath. A dark figure emerged from the pitched blackness and stared.

Jim Casey was having coffee and sorting through some papers as Laura appeared from the elevator. She looked surprisingly tired and slightly pale. He watched her as she approached and sat across from him. She seemed vacant, almost dazed. He wiped the scone crumbs from his mouth before he spoke. "You okay?"

She seemed unsure how to answer and it took her several moments before she replied. She rolled her head on her shoulders. "I don't know...I feel so drained. Like the life has been sucked out of me. I was fine going to bed...but..."
He stared with genuine concern.
"But...what?"

She rubbed her eyes and took a deep breath. "But I feel... almost... violated in some way. Like every part of my body has been clawed. Maybe the last few days are catching up with me." She shook her head as if to fully wake and he tried to reassure her. "That's understandable. Look... I hope you don't mind but I've cleared my diary for the day and I'd like to take you out... if you're okay with that."

She managed a smile. "Is this a date?" For the first time since she'd met him, Jim Casey seemed almost insecure. He shifted uneasily.
"I'd like to think so."

Her smile widened as she scanned his face. "You're blushing...you do know that?" He sprang straight back to full confidence and replied without thinking. "That'll be the whiskey from the wedding... note to self... blood pressure and double malt rarely mix." She laughed and he greatly enjoyed that she did. They left the lobby as the morning light beamed through the reception windows.

The sun was still shining down as throngs of tourists milled about the great coastline. Jim and Laura were at the highest point of the Cliffs as the edged sandstone walls lead down to the ocean like a stairway from the Gods. She had an ice cream cone in one hand and, when she wasn't looking, he leaned in to take a bite. She dabbed him on the face and he relished the sound of her laughter. They walked along the stone slabs that lined the length of the cliffs and he pointed to the clear blue horizon. She recorded on her phone and he even posed for a picture. It was fun that came as a relief to Laura and she took in the sea air like she was breathing for the very first time.

They walked further along the trail and he gave a brief lesson in history. They were called Moher after a fort that had once stood on Hags Head. The head itself was a thing of pure folklore. Carved by The Cailleach, the Witch of Winter, as her eyes on the ocean, the face was her representation cut into the bedrock of Namurian Shale and Sandstone. That it was a natural anomaly meant little against the weight of fantasy.

The walls dropped some 750ft straight down to meet the froth and spray of the wild Atlantic and, as you stared out across the waves, the next landmass to greet you would be Labrador, Newfoundland. He extended his hand to the ocean.
"You came here looking for answers and here they are. Brady by name but Irish by the grace of God."

She was taken by the moment and speech abandoned her. She looked at him with such curiosity and when she did speak, it was deliberately light-hearted. "Are you sure you're not an attorney. Back home we have to ward them off with garlic, you know."

He rolled up his sleeves. "Like I said... no Rolex. I'm just a country boy, harvest moon and dungarees." She looked at the grey in his temples and the age lines about his eyes.
"It's been a while since you were a boy... but you've aged well."

He clapped his hands together and beamed. "Hey... that was a compliment. You're going sweet on me. Let me buy you dinner and I'll tell you about life in a small town." She put her phone away and he took her hand as they walked back toward the visitors centre.

CHAPTER SIX: ALL THE FALLEN ANGELS

'And I looked, and behold, a pale horse!
And its rider's name was Death,
and Hell followed with him'
Revelation 6:8

They had made their way along the coast and stopped at the same fishing village tavern as they'd visited before. Jim was keeping an eye out for the incoming trawlers and he desperately wanted to avoid Bo Chen Yang if at all possible.

He liked Yang but he just felt that Laura had endured enough already and conversations of cadavers should, ideally, be kept to one a week. They were enjoying soup with fresh rolls and the conversation was flowing. She was updating him on the past. "Those letters are heartbreaking...and terrifying."

Jim buttered a bread roll and dunked it into his soup. "Certainly sounds that way. I knew Edward went to war... but I didn't know what happened over there." He stuffed the soggy roll into his mouth and wiped the drips away with a napkin as she watched. She took a moment to recall events. "Whatever they found in those mountains really affected him." Jim stopped eating and considered what she'd just said and he spoke with intensity. "The man in those letters was not the man we knew in Drumasheen. Edward Brady was a frightening individual and the town simply avoided him. My heart always went out to his daughters...he owned them...like cattle. No wonder Kathleen went mad." He raised his hand in apology before she had time to admonish him.

A waiter arrived with two bowls of Irish stew and placed them on the table. They thanked him and Laura picked up where they'd left off. "There's one letter left but I don't believe it's from Edward. The handwriting is different. There may be more in the house." He choose his words carefully and he was understanding in his approach. "You came looking for answers and you got some, at least. Perhaps you're better off leaving it now."

She sipped on a soda water and dried her lips. She nodded ever so slowly but spoke with conviction. "I've been around the block a time or two. For most of my life, the only characters I could connect with were the ones I created in my novels. They were like friends to me in a sense. I never really felt I belonged anywhere or with anyone." She composed herself before she continued. "I had a few relationships over the years but I simply couldn't settle. I was always searching for something that I could never find... and I looked for things in people that they simply couldn't offer."

Her voice became softer and he noticed again that she thumbed the scar on her wrist without knowing it. "It was lonely... at times. But I knew that someday... someday before I died, I'd get my answers... all of them... and, when that happened, I'd be complete... alone probably... but completely alone and that, in itself, is a goal worth fighting for."

The waiter came to the table and asked if they needed a dessert menu. They declined with Jim saying he was sweet enough. When they were alone again, looked to her with great compassion. "I'm just concerned, that's all." She accepted that wholeheartedly and, when she smiled, there was a fondness in it. "And what of you... a broken marriage can't have been easy." It wasn't something he'd been asked too often of late and he really had to think about it. "No... it wasn't." He raised his eyebrows and blew hard. "I think the hardest part was hurting someone that I deeply cared for. In leaving, I had brought sadness to someone I'd vowed to protect and it went against every ounce of who I was... still does." He sat, head bowed and bare but she persisted.

"If you loved her, why did you leave?"

He sipped on his cappuccino and stared past her. "We'd married young... and by the time it was over, we'd grown into two entirely different people. I think she missed the man I used to be just as much as I yearned for the girl I walked down the aisle with, but she'd turned into her mother and I'd turned into this... and we started resenting each other for those changes." He looked directly at her now. "It didn't seem right... we still had lives to live." He noticed their cups were empty so he went inside for refills.

When he came back, she was facing the ocean and standing in its breeze. Her eyes were closed but she was aware of him. "I'm sorry if I appear to pry. I just think you've been carrying that guilt for just a few years too many." She opened her eyes and turned to him "If you have a life to live... then go and live it. Can't be easy in a small town."

He snapped back to being upbeat and cynical. "Small towns are like zombie movies. Twisted aul' fellas shuffling out of the dark asking where you come from or who your people are... bastards would live in your ear." He cocked his finger like a revolver. "Always aim for the head... or the bladder... common problem areas." He shoots off a volley. She looked across the street to where the fishing boats were coming in. Bo Chen Yang was hauling nets when he saw her and waved. She waved back.

Later that evening, Laura came looking for Shane Kelly. She had a printed and bound a manuscript of 'The Olive Grove' which she wanted him to have. The receptionist said that Kelly hadn't been to work in a day or two but he said he was, most probably, curled up at home reading 'The Night Before Dawn' for the tenth time and she noted how sweet it was of Laura to write such a message. "He's shown it to everyone" The receptionist told her "You really lifted his spirits." She suggested Laura try again in a day or so and she said she would leave a message for Kelly if he should surface sooner.

Laura was towel drying her hair following a hot shower. She stood in front of a full length mirror attached to the wardrobe door and she bent over so that her hair fall forward. There were scuff marks on the wooden floor and she noticed them for the first time. There appeared to be traces of dried mud that trailed, in spots, all the way to the foot of her bed. She followed them with her eyes and, as she did, the wardrobe door creaked all the way open and smacked her on the buttocks. It startled her and she shot up, pulling the towel from her hair. She closed the closet door and felt it latch. She tugged at it and it appeared secure but she rang reception and asked if maintenance might take a look the following day.

When she was comfortable, she opened her laptop and keyed in the word 'Iblis'. Several sites appeared with the headings Devil, Djinn and Shaytan. It was 'The Fallen Angel', 'Desolation', 'The Corrupter' and when she searched for images, she was shocked by the ferocity of the beast. There were images of despair, death, centuries of suffering and sacrifice... and of the odious evil that was The Iblis itself. It was the winged serpent, the unclean spirit, demon of the damned and a devourer of lost children. She recoiled in absolute horror and closed her laptop.

She poured a Baileys and sifted through the letters and photos. She came to the last letter and, very reluctantly, she opened it. There were many pages but she read:

'Occupied Territories,
Ottoman Empire.
Feb 2nd 1916
Dear Father Tiernan,

DELPHINE

My name is Francis Dargan and I have served proudly on the battlefields of Gallipoli with your friend and parishioner, Edward Brady. He mentioned you many times when we were camped near Bigali and he talked often of what a tremendous support you have been to his family back home. It is for this reason, and because of your unwavering devotion to the Lord Almighty, that I ask you pay full attention to contents of this letter. On the morning of January 15th, our troops were ordered over the top and we charged into the din to an unknown fate. Several of us, including Edward, found safety in a trench and we engaged the enemy from there.'

There was screaming from everywhere. Smoke billowed across the battlefield and shells pounded the mud. Francis Dargan and Edward Brady were side by side. Several other men crouched down around them. They rose up and opened fire before, once again, taking cover. A shell came over and Brady pushed Dargan out of its path to protect him. It exploded in their midst with a deafening blast. Francis Dargan was blown backwards.

As the smoke cleared, Edward Brady was slumped over and bloodied beyond recognition. Dargan went to him in a desperate attempt to stem the flow. Brady was bleeding out everywhere and shock had set in. He grabbed Dargan in raw panic but his grip was weak, he gave several quick gasps and he slumped into his arms. His head rested on his comrades' chest and he went still.

Dargan closed Brady's eyes and lowered him into the mud as a troupe of men came over the top in a hurried retreat. They were shouting in panic as gunfire blasted out everywhere. Dargan joined them but he looked back one last time to witness the body of Edward Brady being trampled deeper into a stagnant pool. He ran into no man's land and in the direction of his camp as the shells exploded around him.

Daylight was fading but Laura was unaware of it. She was immersed in the letter. She turned to another page and continued.

'I made it back to safety and reported Edwards fate to our commanding officer. Edwards widow would have been notified had we been in a position to do so but we were disconnected from the world before us and cut off from the path behind. All we could do was wait. Twelve days passed before we could advance once more. I found myself in the same trench where I had left Edward. What happened next will stay with me long after the screams of my comrades have faded.'

Dargan was surrounded by the corpses of fallen soldiers. There was an overpowering stench of decay but he held his breath when he could and he dragged them aside in search of his comrade. He saw a shoulder sticking from the mud and began digging with his hands. He managed to pull Edwards head above the sludge and he was trying to free the rest of his body when there was a sound unlike the others. It reminded him of a low flying plane but it was different. The drone intensified until even the sound of shelling was drowned out. Soldiers were looking to the sky but visibility was hampered by smoke from shells and the bodies of burning men.

Suddenly, through the smoke, a monstrous swarm of flies plummeted downward, sending Francis scurrying through the bodies for sanctuary. The flies swarmed around the remains of Edward Brady making their entry through mouth, nostrils and ears. They plunged into the bloody pools around him and covered him in a thick black paste. The buzzing eventually died out and the flies lay still. There was a deep gurgle from the dead throat of Private Brady, followed by a woeful groaning as his corpse emerged from the thick mud. To the horror of Dargan and the others, Brady sat upright and began to pull himself from the mire. The flies fell away in their thousands as he rose up.

Francis Dargan came sprinting across no man's land screaming. Shells exploded around him and the smoke clouds are fog-like and thick but Francis made it into a clearing and saw his troupe in the distance. He raced to them and attempted to speak but fear and exhaustion prohibited this. As he finally found words, he saw that the entire battalion were lined up in silence and staring beyond him. He turned and looked. Edward Brady was walking through the fog with shells exploding all round him. He did not flinch. He was caked in mud and blood but his boots pounded the scorched earth as he marched forward in defiance. A shell exploded mere feet in front of him but Brady emerged through the smoke untouched and unfazed. The men parted as he approached. No words were spoken. He walked through them to a tent where he laid down on a bunk and fell straight to asleep.

The winter's night had descended and a silence had fallen outside of Laura's window. She opened a soda water and drank from it. She put the bottle down and continued with the letter.

> *'He has been silent ever since but that music box plays throughout the night and, there are moments in the dark when I feel Edwards spirit is somehow trying to warn us from the great beyond. I am sorry to startle you so. As a man of God, I am sure this is difficult for you to accept. I would hardly believe it myself were it not that I was witness to it. I am compelled to inform you as I had made a commitment to Edward that I would contact you should tragedy befall him and befall him it did. In fulfilment of that commitment the n, I will ask that you continue to offer Anna Brady the support in the future that you have freely given in the past and I implore you to offer prayer and protection to all of those who should ever fall under this creatures control.*
>
> *Yours in grief,*
> *Private Francis Dargan'*

DELPHINE

Laura folded the letter and placed it back in its envelope with great care. She closed her eyes and sighed. She took a moment to let the story sink in. She reached for the ledger and stopped, unsure as to whether she really wanted to know its content. Eventually she opened it to find pages of newspaper clippings. She was tired and she merely turned the pages and scanned the headlines.

> *'Obituary - Father Michael Tiernan - Drumasheen – Perished in jaunting tragedy.' Dated 1923'*
> *'Mystery as twin girls vanish'. Dated 1931*
> *'Tragedy in Drumasheen as girl, 9, disappears'. Dated 1947*
> *'Sadness as search called off for missing child'. Dated 1963*
> *'Missing Limerick man still not found'. Dated 1969*
> *'Mystery of the Missing Mary's. Friends disappear on school outing.' Dated 1986*
> *'Holiday tragedy as girl, 12, goes missing'. Dated 2009*
> *'Suicide in Drumasheen. Grieving father drowns'. Dated 2010'*

Laura could take no more. She went to the mini bar and removed several small whiskey bottles. She poured a stiff drink and stared at the table.

The weather man had said the good spell wouldn't last and he was as good as his word. On the day of the funeral, black clouds had waded in and, though the heavy rain was holding off, it was showery and miserable. The funeral itself was poorly attended. Other than Laura and Jim, there were a few stragglers that may have known Eileen or may just as well have stepped in out of the rain. Laura noted that Shane Kelly was absent and it was customary in small towns for hoteliers and publicans to attend such occasions and do their best to look sombre. Jim had said, in one of his 'small towns Do's and Don'ts' that, when it came to funerals, 'anyone with an eatery or a drinking hole would prostitute their arses by shuffling round a church looking morose, shaking hands and consoling the family like they genuinely gave a shit.' Obviously Eileen wasn't worth the performance and Laura felt bad for the old lady that, even in death, she was alone.

In the cemetery, the rain decided not to delay the inevitable a moment further and the skies finally opened. As Eileen was lowered down, Laura noticed a mourner in the distance by a tall grey pillar. She wore a bonnet with a veil and she looked diminutive by such a robust monument. Laura asked Jim who she was and, glancing over, he whispered "I wasn't sure she'd come. That's Kathleen, Eileen's sister." When Laura looked over again, Kathleen was gone. Laura walked to where she had stood and looked about but she had left. As she turned to go, she noted the inscriptions on great pillar.

DELPHINE

'Erected in memory of the missing.
Molly & Nellie Wilmott - Twins - 1931
Anne Lynch - 1947
Carmel Hogan - 1963
Private John Allman (Sarsfield Barracks) - 1969
Mary Tobin & Mary Knowles - 1986
Katie Markham - 2009
May God keep them warm.'

Other names were added but Laura knew that these were, at least some of those mentioned in the paper clippings. The rain was channelled down along each letter of the inscription and she was compelled to run the tips of her fingers across it. She went to Jim who was waiting by the front of the church. "I might go to the house later and see if I can't find more photos." He slipped a key off his bunch and handed it to her. "I'd tell you to avoid the place but you wouldn't listen. I might be with you after 4 so I'll see you in the hotel I'm free." She agreed and they left.

1923: The house was in darkness except for a light from the downstairs living room. A horse drawn jaunting car appeared from the road and made its way up the avenue. There was a single occupant, the horse stalled by the front door and a darkly dressed figure dismounted. The figure went to the window and the emanating light gave a clearer definition. It was a priest. He pulled the collar of his coat up to meet his black fedora hat and he shivered at the intense cold. There was movement inside so he went to the door and knocked. He heard footsteps on the tiled hallway floor and Anna opened the door. She was pale and worn and, even in the dim light, he could see the dark circles under her eyes. But she was pleased to see him and she welcomed him instantly. "Father Tiernan, so good of you to call. Come in." He removed his hat and walked past her toward the living-room. The door closed.

Edward Brady was slumped into the fireside armchair. There was a blanket across him and it was pulled up to his chest. His head leaned to one side and his eyes were blank as he stared at the flames. There was a box camera on the ground beside him and a music box sat to the centre of a drawing room coffee table. The door opened and Anna appeared with Tiernan close behind. He stood by Edward and produced a small glass bottle from his coat pocket. It was filled with holy water. He poured several drops onto his fingers and pressed them to Edwards temple. He made the sign of a cross and he scrutinized Edward closely. He leaned in and spoke but maintained his glare. "Edward... it's Father Tiernan." There was no response and Edward did not move.

Anna spoke softly and there was a bleak despair in her words. "There's no point. He's not in there, you see... and I doubt that he ever will be again." Tiernan is still assessing Edward and he noticed that Anna was confused by his inspection. To deflect her attention he reached down and picked up the camera. "That's nice. I'd thought about buying one." Anna stood behind Edward and rested her hand on his shoulder. "We live now only by our memories." She indicates to the camera. "Would you mind Father?" He walked to the front. He snapped the photo and put the camera on the table next to the music box.

Before speaking again the priest composed himself. "Anna... I need to discuss something with you." He removed a letter from the inside pocket of his overcoat and thumbed it nervously. "Perhaps we could talk in the kitchen... over tea." Anna sensed a gravity to his voice so she left the room with Tiernan in tow. Edward Brady remained slumped in his seat. A bead of holy water trickled down the length of his cheek and his eye twitched.

Anna was seated at the kitchen table with Tiernan sitting across from her. The pages of a letter were on the table by Tiernan's pipe and tobacco pouch. She was blank and he could see that she was struggling. Her voice was just above a whisper. "So... you're telling me that my husband is what...the Devil?" He rested his hand on hers and spoke with some conviction. "I'm telling you that Francis Dargan believed your husband died out there... that he witnessed... an abomination." He stood up and paced "I didn't believe it either until he came to see me. I've never seen a more terrified creature in all my life." She got up from the table and opened the kitchen door. "I think it's best that you leave now Father." She became distraught. "My husband needs a doctor for Gods sake... not an exorcist... oh why can't somebody just help me?" She cried in desperation and exhaustion.

Tiernan was desperately trying to get through to her. "Anna, you read the letter. Edward was buried in the mud for twelve days... twelve days! That's not your husband in there... and I'm here to warn you... please be careful." She held the door open wider and there was a purpose in her voice now. "Leave!"

Forgetting his pipe & pouch, he walked slowly by her and let himself out.

Anna was startled by the sound of a music box coming from the Living-room. She made her way down the hallway and stopped.

She called out but there is no reply. She opened the door and nervously stared inside. The music box was open and, as it played, the porcelain ballerina pirouetted with grace. The armchair was empty except for a blanket resting on its arm. Edward was gone. Laura looked about in panic and called out but, again, there is no reply. She ran to the kitchen but found it empty. Then she heard a shuffling upstairs and she rushed upward still calling out her husband's name.

She reached the top of the stairs and was stunned to find Edward Brady standing at the end of the upper hallway. He had his back to her and he was facing a bedroom door. He stood entirely still but she could hear a deep rasp on his breath. She approached him cautiously. Her voice was a whimper as she calls out. "Edward?" He did not respond. She edged closer and the rasp intensified. She reached out and her fingers made contact.

The rasp stopped and he slowly turned. His face was taut and yellow and his eyes were entirely rolled back in their sockets. His mouth stretched open repulsively to reveal a thick wall of flies that crawled from within and swarmed about his features. Anna reeled backward and screamed. Edward roared out in fury and his eyes rolled forward so that they were burning into her. He lunged but she escaped him briefly and scrambled to the stairs.

She was three steps down when he grabbed her by the hair and yanked her back. He dragged her along the hallway and kicked open a bedroom door. He threw her violently inside and slipped his braces off. He began unbuttoning his trousers as she pleaded for mercy "Please... no... please Jesus Christ.. Edward...No!" He stepped into the bedroom and slammed the door closed behind him. The house was filled with muffled screams and the melody of a music box.

Father Tiernan made his way toward home as his horse and cart ambled along. There was a full moon and its faint light lead the way. He pulled slightly on the reigns and the horse came to a standing stop.
Tiernan reached into his pocket as he addressed the animal.
"Time for a smoke my old friend." He searched through his coat pockets and it dawned on him that he'd left the Brady house without his pipe and pouch. He pondered the situation momentarily and decided that the wrath of Anna Brady would be less painful than the ache of his addiction.

He turned the cart around and headed back. He turned onto the avenue of the Brady house and noted that the front door was open. A faint hallway light was visible.

As he neared the property, the pace of his cart slowed and his horse ground to a halt.

The animal seemed anxious and uncertain. It took several steps back and tossed its head as it neighed out to the night sky. Tiernan tapped it with his harness and encouraged it forward. "Come on boy... giddy up." But the animal refused and its distress became more acute. Tiernan looked up ahead and saw a solitary figure appeared through the open door onto the avenue. It was hunched over as it shuffled toward him. As the figure came into view, Tiernan was stunned to find that it was Anna Brady. Her clothes were ripped and she held the breast of her blouse up to cover her bare bosom. She was badly bruised and blood ran from her mouth and nostrils. Tiernan was horrified and he rose up. "Mother of God..."
The priest was unaware of the dark shape the rose up ominously behind him. The dark of Edward Brady towered over him and, as the horse neighed in abject terror, Brady grabbed him around the throat and began to throttle him.

Tiernan tried to fight back but he was no match to Brady's ferocious strength. Brady's fingers locked tight as Anna called out and Edward stood completely still. "Leave him be... leave him... and I will stay."

Her lips were badly swollen and her words were mumbled. "Let him go... and I will be yours...always. Edward considered the proposal. He looked from Anna to Tiernan and back. He tossed Tiernan back into his seat and dismounted. He walked to Anna and she cowered before him.

DELPHINE

Father Tiernans voice surprised them both. Tiernan rose up once more and held a bible forward. There was fire and brimstone in his words. "Behold, I cast out demons in the name of our Lord Jesus Christ. I know who you are beast and I have come to destroy you. You will flee as smoke is driven and you will melt amongst the wicked legions that burn in the fires of God. I cast you out!" He grabbed the bible in both hands and thrust it forward. "Out Belial... out!!!"

Edward opened his mouth. It stretched to a breaking point and there was the sound of bone dislocating. His jaw snapped sideways and a swarm gushed forth, attacking the horse and sending it into a frenzy. The animal bolted and Tiernan was thrown backwards. In a mighty gallop the horses took off down the avenue. It careered onto the road and they watched as the jaunting cart smashed over and was dragged away.

Tiernans body laid strewn on the roadside and Anna ran to him. He was gurgling through his own blood as he reached for her hand and she gently stroked his face as he slipped away.

CHAPTER SEVEN: LIFTING THE VEIL

'Only three things cannot stay hidden, the sun, the moon and the truth.'
Buddha - Philosopher & Spiritual Teacher

The lobby clock at The Burren Arms was one of those nautically themed timepieces described as 'Coastal'. It was a ships wheel in brass with a wooden inlay that sported a map of the ocean with 'There be monsters' inscribed just above a Cthulhu or a Kraken. Laura hadn't figured out which one it was even though she'd paced by that clock for almost an hour. She'd approached the receptionist earlier to see if Jim Casey had left a message but he hadn't been in contact. It was 4.30pm now and the daylight was fading. If she was to go, it would have to be now. She approached the receptionist one more time but there was still no news. As she walked away, Laura turned and asked of someone else. "Have you heard from Mr Kelly at all?" The receptionist shook her head but Laura noted a deep concern and it was one she shared entirely.

The drive out to the house was testing at best. Laura had missed a turn or two and, by the time she pulled into the avenue, the dark of night had fallen. The car came to a stop just past the house and she caught the place from a gable end so that she could see the land behind. A full moon shimmered on the lakes surface and she felt a cold chill as it did. She focused only on that house as she approached and she listened to the arms of the oak tree as they creaked in the wind but she did not divert her eyes. She climbed the porch steps and removed the key from the watch pocket of her jeans. The locked turned without a fight and the door swung slowly open.

She could make out the stairs to her right but the rest was just blackness. She stepped inside and reached for a light switch. The bulb flickered and came alive as a dim glow that allowed her make her way around. She went to the bottom of the stairs and stared up.

Laura was surprised to find that the light in the upper hallway also worked. Again, the light was dim at best, but it was more than she had hoped for and she made her way to the bedroom closet quickly. She retrieved the hat box and went to the bedroom window to where Delphine stood closed and still.

She was almost at the top of the stairs when the upper hall light flickered and failed. She took three steps down before she looked back and it was then she heard it. The wind had whipped up and the windows rattled a little but there was another sound in there. It was more than that. It was a collective, several sounds pitched together ... voices ... whispers. She listened as they became clearer and she stared into the dark for the source. The voices were childlike and the whispers were a garbled mix of pleas and warnings. Some begged for clemency while others were angry and defiant. Suddenly a door banged downstairs and the house went entirely silent bar the whistling of the wind.

The hat box yielded more than just photos. As she sat at the kitchen table, Laura found that the photos to the top were just another cover for what laid underneath. She had discovered a map of Turkey highlighting the hamlet of Bigali and the hills above it. There were a series of circles in pen and she identified them as search boundaries by the notes scribbled beside them. The words 'Şeytanın Beşiği' were written in red ink with a series of question marks and, across the bottom, she read the words 'Shaytan said "You created me from fire. Adam is no more than clay so I will not prostrate before him. Allow mere spite until the day of resurrection. "So he was taken then to Şeytanın Beşiği where the lord placed him beyond the hands of clay and men.'

There were names scribbled on a sheet of faded writing paper. Umut Batuk and Yusuf Alpman. There was a handwritten map of a street in the Dardanelles city of Çanakkale with a corner building circled and öbür dünya written beside it and the name HASSAN written in block capitals. She keyed öbür dünya into her phone and Googled. It was Turkish for 'After Life' but, when she added the city name, she discovered that öbür dünya was a specialist antiquity shop in Çanakkale and the search pinpointed it to exactly where it was on the handwritten map. Allowing for the fade on the paper, Laura suspected the map predated search engines by many years.

She was still investigating when she heard them again. The whispers were coming from the stairs and there was a panic to them, a fear that she felt run through her. She rose from the table and slowly started toward the hallway. As she edged forward, she could see their outlines on the steps but, despite her sense of dread, still she inched closer. They were dotted on the stairway like Russian dolls, each one a step higher than the other. Just children... young girls whose lives were taken long before they bloomed. Faces filled with sadness and voices that pleaded and implored with such desperation. She stood facing them in silence and, as their sadness overcame her, she wept. Her whole body was trembling when a door under the stairs popped open and, for just a second, she could see the face of little Marie as she whispered one word..."Delphine". She faded out but the moment was defined by the melody of the music box as it drifted from the kitchen. Laura closed the broom cupboard door and turned toward the lullaby. She froze on the spot as fear consumed her.

At that very moment, the light blew in the kitchen and she was aware of his presence. He stood by the window with his back to her but she could make out his reflection on the sink window as the dim hall light still offered some illumination. As she backed away, she could see the children disappear in single file and that's when he turned.

He was tall and skeletal and his funeral suit draped from him like a clothes horse. His eyes burned with pure hate and his flesh was ravaged to partly expose teeth and bone. He began to glide forward, slowly at first, and she ran as the hallway light flickered and went out.

She'd made it to the door but the lock was sticking and she struggled with it. Panic had taken over and she cried out as the lock turned but the door still defied her. Finally it relented but, as she attempted to flee, he appeared from the dark and locked his arm around her throat in a vice-like grip. Her screams did not find a clemency and her struggles were in vain as he was utterly in control. He drifted backward with his capture until they were almost lost to the dark. Laura was losing consciousness and a wave of futility had silenced her. This was the place and now was the time.

She had come here in search of her past and, now she would die at its hands. She watched as the night swirled in around her and her legs gave way. Then, when all was lost, the door burst open and the moonlight flooded into the hallway as Kathleen Brady rushed forward screaming "Get your hands off her you bastard!" Laura was released but, as she fell to the floor, she passed out and landed with a thud.

When she woke, Laura was surprised to find herself in strange settings. She was lying on a strange sofa in a strange room and Kathleen was putting the final touches to a hot whiskey. She sat up and took a long sip while she looked around. The cottage was small but had a character, a delightfully old world enchantment that was rather striking. Kathleen came to her side and stroked her hair. She had dispensed with her bonnet and Laura could see her clearly for the first time.
Her grey hair was shoulder length and, though her features had submitted to time, her pale blue eyes were so filled with affection that Laura felt immediately at ease. Her voice was soothing to her. "Do you remember what

DELPHINE

happened?" Laura was still groggy but she recalled the ordeal and nodded. "That was Edward, wasn't it?" Kathleen answered her question with a question. "Did you read the letters that I left for you?" Again Laura nodded and Kathleen continued. "Well, then you'll know that Edward died a very, very long time ago and he lives now only through Delphine."

She propped up a pillow before she continued "Did he warn you?" Laura looked totally confused so Kathleen clarified the question. "Did Delphine play before that creature appeared?" Laura was clear now. "Yes...yes it did." Kathleen smiled and brushed the hair from Laura's cheeks.

"That, my dear, was Edward. The box is like a Dybuk only filled with rapture and raw emotion. It warns us... against the other." Laura wanted to know what 'the other' actually was so Kathleen obliged.

She told Laura that the Iblis was as ancient as time. It was The Butcher of Herod who killed the first born, it rode ahead of Genghis Khan as the Mongols laid waste to Asia, it was torturer to the Spanish Inquisition, it raped in the hulls of slave ships and lynched in the old bayous. She said that the Turks even believed it was the devil incarnate, Shaytan, and they feared its wrath as absolutely as they accepted its existence. But it wasn't Shaytan. It was something even worse. It was yet another fallen angel of God, an even more detestable force in the universe that challenged both the Lords of light and darkness and together they had entombed it in the holy mountain. "I went to Bigali after I was released from hospital" Kathleen told her "and I spoke with the Imams. They said that it was incarcerated in that fortress...but Edward and the others set it free." She told Laura that she searched for answers in Bigali but had found only more questions. She said that only one person knew the actual location of Şeytanın Beşiği and her name was Umut Batuk but she had vanished many years earlier and would be of a great age if she still lived. She'd had a spiritual defender, a confessor by the name Yusuf Alpman who protected her from sinister elements that had long plagued the family and he had purchased certain items from an antiques dealer called Hassan Yildrim who owned a small corner store called öbür dünya in the city of Çanakkale. Kathleen said she had gone to that city and found the store but lady there had never heard of Hassan or Yusuf and she ran out of leads at that point.

Laura digested everything as she finished her whiskey. She put the glass down and turned to Kathleen. "It was terrified of you... the Iblis I mean." Kathleen took her hand and held it gently. "It feeds on purity... all those poor children. It violates and corrupts but absolute love is unbearable to something so wicked. It wasn't terrified of me... it was repelled by the devotion I have for you." She put her hand to her chest and her breathing became erratic. "You must excuse me for a moment sweetheart, I need to take my medication." Kathleen rebuffed Laura's offer of assistance and disappeared into a back room while Laura took in the house. She opened a bedroom door and looked inside.

Laura was stunned by the sight. The room is almost a shrine to her and the walls were adorned with pictures of her growing up overseas. There were photos of every gift she'd ever received and copies of her novels have been stacked neatly on the shelves. On the bedside table, there is a miniature music box and, when she opened it, another ballerina pirouetted to another sweet waltz. Kathleen walked in behind her. "We all got one you see. My mother insisted we carry it with us... but there was ever only one that really spoke to us. It's pretty though. I suppose she couldn't allow him to inflict such cruelty without easing the pain... and it was cruel... and heartless. It took my life from me." Her memories overwhelmed her as they had done so many times before. Laura attempted to console her but it was years too late for that. Still, she tried. "Yes... Marie. I'm so sorry."

Kathleen shook her head and when she spoke, it was barely above a whimper. "Marie was not my child... she was Eileen's." Kathleen went to her bedside table and removed a single photo from the top drawer.

It showed a young Kathleen with a handsome soldier. They were holding a baby. She handed the photo to Laura. "He was such a good man... your father. I loved him very much. He said he would take us away from here... my soldier boy. Then he just vanished like all the others. The Iblis wouldn't share us with anyone, you see. We were just for him." The tears spilled over again. "We were the products of rape and Eileen was not spared.

Marie was a child of incest and savagery. I threatened to take you away so he held little Marie in the lake until she stopped kicking and he told me he would do the same to you if I ever tried to free you from him. He murdered his own child."

Laura was spinning and reality was hitting her in waves so overwhelming that she could drown at any second. Kathleen continued regardless. After all these years, this had to come out. "Then that vile creature took you from me and gave you to Eileen... like a doll. She would never have left, you see, she was weak... damaged... and you were his gift to her for what he'd done to Marie." She took a deep breath and calmed a little. "I was shunned and no one would listen so I came to the house and I took you back. I got you to safety and I didn't care anymore. I tried to burn the place with him in it so that he would never find you but they had me locked away."

Laura looked about the room at the books and the photos. "It was you all along... the gifts." Kathleen is trembling but focused. "Oh yes. You were my baby... my heart and my soul and if I couldn't have all of you, then you'd have a little piece of me." A panic set in and Kathleen started ushering Laura toward the door. "Now I beg you to go back or the sacrifice will be for nothing. You were the one that got away and he won't rest until he has you." The panic spread to Laura and the truth hit like a steam train. "Oh my God... oh my God... I can't take this. I wish I'd never come here!!"

Kathleen moved her to the door and handed her the car keys for the rental. "The figures in black... they want to help you but they have no power in that house unless you call for them. They need your anger. If you leave now, you won't need them. Your car is outside. Run Laura... run and never look back." Laura sprinted across the gravel stones and into the car. She took off like her life depended on it.

Jim Casey had listened to everything she'd had to say and when Laura was finished, he sat back and tried to make some sense of it all. He watched the fishing trawlers as they set off for sea and they sat in silence until a waiter arrived with two tall lattes and plates of eggs benedict. When he'd done, Jim stirred his coffee and spoke up. "So what do you do now?" She was quick to answer. "I get my ass back to Canada where I belong. The next flight is tomorrow night and I intend to be on it." He found a certain sorrow in this and she heard it when he spoke. "Of course. For what it's worth... I will miss you." She gently placed her hand on his. "And I you. I know you won't accept this but you're a good man." He stared at her for several moments. "You wouldn't say that if you knew me. Personally...I'm not Jim Casey's biggest fan. We had a falling out some time ago... never really got past it." She sat back and sipped her latte. "Oh I don't know... I've grown to like him." She sensed his unease and changed the subject. "What will happen to the house?"

He finished his eggs benedict and wiped his mouth. "Well...strictly speaking that's your call but I'd knock it to the ground." She got her jacket on and collected her shoulder bag. "Sounds like a plan. I'll be in touch as soon as I hit Burlington. I'd like to stay in contact if that's okay." He smiled and nodded as they stopped by the car and watched the trawlers go about their business. She eyed him without his knowledge and it was the first time in many years that she felt the profound pang of loss. "I have some things to do today... but, perhaps we could meet for drinks this evening." He jumped right back in. "Second date in a week... I haven't been this lucky since I had all my own teeth." They sat into the car and disappeared out the Drumasheen Road.

1939: It was a summer's day and the sun had laid a blanket of heat over every living thing. Dragonflies darted from bush to bush but, even on such a glorious afternoon, the front of the house looked neglected and the great oak that once stood proudly was tired and weary now. Two young girls, perhaps five or six, were playing on the porch steps and they marvelled at the maiden of the music box as she spun slowly to the chimes of Elgar's Salut d'Amour Op.12. They are wearing summer dresses decorated with the images of a carnival, elephants and carousels a-plenty. The girls took up position and slowly drifted into the waltz.

The door opened and Anna Brady appeared. She was older now, if not a little browbeaten by the world. She carried an old box camera which she placed on the porch when she knelt to embrace them. She kissed the first child. "My sweet Kathleen." and then the other "My lovely

DELPHINE

Eileen...two sides of a mothers heart." Kathleen was curious about the ballerina. "Mother, why did you call her Delphine?"

Anna drifted a little "It was the name given to her by someone I used to know... someone I wish you'd gotten to know." Sensing their confusion, she took the camera and walked out front. "One for the photo album." As she snapped, the gaunt figure of Edward Brady appeared in the doorway. He was wearing a black suit with waistcoat and his eyes were sunken back. He glared at the photographer.

Eileen was shy of the lens while Kathleen was defiant of it. The moment was captured forever. Edward stepped forward so that the light exposed his true menace. His face was little more than a thinly covered skull and his lips were peeled back to reveal teeth that were blackened and broken.

There was an overwhelming fear that stunned Anna to silence. He eyed the children as they danced. He looked from Eileen to Kathleen and back to Eileen. He made his selection. Edward reached down and yanked the girls apart before hoisting Eileen up. He turned and headed for the stairs with the child screaming out for help. Anna rushed up behind him and pounded her fists upon him. "No! No Edward...please...No!"

He turned and stared with such malice that even Anna's anger was stunted. He leaned in close and whispered into her ear. As he did, Kathleen collapsed on the front step and began to spasm. Her body contorted into a rigid arch and a froth dripped from both corners of her mouth so that her breathing was compromised. Anna ran to her in outright panic as Edward climbed the stairs with Eileen still screaming from under his arm.

Limerick City was more like home than anything Laura had found in West Clare. It was that bustling hub brimming with angry urbanites who would rather walk over you than make way for you to pass. For all the warmth she'd found in the townlands around Drumasheen, she found herself negotiating buses and busy thoroughfares without as much as a 'Howdy'.

She had Google open on her phone and she was looking at a Moroccan Trinket shop called Marrakech which had an address in the city centre. She wandered up William Street but alleyways led to passageways and into old lanes and, before long, she was hopelessly lost. She asked a stranger for help and was directed to where she needed to be.

Marrakech had all the hallmarks of a Middle Eastern bazaar and one could be forgiven for imagining they were thousands of miles from the South West of Ireland. Thick rugs were stacked up with several hanging from wall brackets that ran ceiling to floor. Leather goods were laid out on counter tops and a variety of pottery and studded jewellery were on display throughout the store. Arabic artistry depicted family life with heavily religious undertones and the burning incense gave the store an odour Moroccan musk that seemed entirely out of place in a Limerick side street.

DELPHINE

As she browsed through the shelves, a young North African man appeared through a beaded curtain and introduced himself as Abbas. Laura wanted to get her terminology right so, once again, she reverted to Google. "Yes... Hi. I'm looking to buy a Nazar... have I pronounced it properly?" She showed him the image on her phone and he nodded. "You pronounced it very well. Most people just ask for amulets."

He removed a tray from under the counter and placed it before her. The tray was filled with eye shaped amulets made from smooth blue glass. Each one has the depiction of a teardrop in the centre. Laura was quite taken with them. "They're very beautiful." He handed her one and she ran her fingers over it. He explains the nature of the Nazar. "They can be used as ornaments... even jewellery... but they are also a powerful protection against the evil eye. That is their place in my culture."

There was a movement from behind the beaded curtain and Laura could make out a figure moving about. Abbas noticed her concern. "That's my grandfather. Please ignore him. He is oldest man in all of my family, the Ishmaelite, and he forgets himself sometimes." Laura waved to the figure behind the curtain but he did not move.

She selected two amulets and, as they were being bagged, she noticed that the grandfather was staring at her blankly through the beads. She paid for her items and was about to leave when the old man shuffled forward. His eyes were locked on her and he was clearly distressed. He began calling out to her. "Laqad laeanuk...laqad laeanuk!"

He became even more distressed and he held his head as he cried out to her. "Allah maeak wayahmik min alshar!"

Laura was scared and upset. She fumbled with her bag as she backed away slowly. Abbas was trying to calm his grandfather but without success. The old man wept openly and raised his hands to heaven. Laura was distraught. "Jesus Christ... what's he saying?"

The young man was ushering his elder behind the beads as he called out to her. "He says that you are cursed and he asks that God may watch over you and protect you. Please leave!" She edged out backwards and pulled the door closed behind her.

Once she was outside in the daylight, she found her way back to the busier roadway and the sound of traffic seemed more appealing now. Her heart was still thumping and she felt somewhat lightheaded so she rested against a wall and watched the world from the outside. She watched as they ran across each other and car horns blasted out and buses filled with weary strangers made their way from one place to another and groups banged shoulders and, in their midst, she was convinced she saw a tall gaunt figure in black weaving in and out of sight. She got her breath and didn't delay in the city any further.

The car trundled along a bumpy road and came to a stop directly outside the cottage. It looked wildly different in daylight and Laura thought it wouldn't look out of place in a
Brothers Grimm collection. Smoke billowed from an old pot chimney at one end of a neatly thatched roof and the

white washed face of the cottage was offset by red painted windows and an exterior half door that remained fully closed. She gathered up the Nazars and approached. She raised her hand to knock but paused for a moment. She could feel her heart thumping in her chest but went ahead and rapped on the half door three times.

Kathleen looked truly disappointed to see her. She shut her eyes tightly before staring at Laura with a great forlorn. She stepped to one side and Laura walked in.

They sat at an old pine table as the turf fire threw flames against the hearth and the shadows flickered on every wall. Laura took the Nazars and handed them to Kathleen. "I read about these in Edward's letters. Those people in Bigali... they believed that this could protect them. Maybe... it could protect us."

Kathleen took the amulets and walked to a side table where there was an old wooden box. She brought the box to Laura and handed it to her. Laura looked inside and found that it was filled with dozens of amulets of all shapes and sizes. Kathleen placed the Nazar with the others and put the lid back on the box. She returned it to its place on the table and then sat by Laura. "I read those letters too."

Kathleen stared at Laura for such a long and silent time. She took in every line and furrow on her face and her eyes were filled with a great affection. She stroked her face. "Look at you..." and the tears came back "oh sweetheart."

She instinctively embraced Laura and Laura found herself compelled to hug back. Tears flowed from both as they embraced. Kathleen leaned back and looked at her again. "When I handed you over... I never thought I'd see you again. It's been all these years. Do you hate me?" She bowed her head but Laura was quick to reassure her. "Oh no... no... never! Why didn't you come with me?" Kathleen held both of Laura's hands. "I had to stay to protect you... to make sure he couldn't find where I'd hidden you. But now you're here and he won't stop until he has you. You must go back.... you do know that." Laura sits back and thought. "I leave tomorrow evening... you could... you could come with me."

Kathleen shook her head and a terrible sadness descended on her. "I remember saying the very same thing to Anna once... and I will answer you as she answered me. As long as that creature is in the house, I must stay." She held Laura's hand with such warmth. "Death will take me... as it did Eileen...but I will find a way... in this world or the next... and you will be safe."

Kathleen got up and stoked the fire. She threw extra turf into the flames and it sparked into a great pyre. She stared at Laura and her expression was far more than just grave. She reached up to the fireplace mantelpiece and took down Edward's music box. She handed it to Laura "I went back for it when the sun was up."

She chose her words carefully. "You must listen to me mo chroí. This music box... you must never leave it far from your sight. No matter where you go... no matter how far you run... the box must go with you. It's the only way you'll know if he's near. He has your scent now...and he will follow that... no matter where you are. Do you understand?"

DELPHINE

Laura looked terrified but Kathleen continued. "Our only hope was Turkey... but I failed. It's not possible to kill this but it's possible to sever it from our family forever... the head from the snake... to send it back to whatever darkness it was born of." She seemed exhausted as she sat back at the table." Those answers have been lost to us now...and all we can do is hope for is that you become just as lost to him...again."

She placed a hand on Laura's shoulder. "Now you know why I did what I did." Laura folded under a flood of fear but she sought the support of her mother's arms. Kathleen comforted her and kissed her head as she slowly rocked from side to side. Laura sat up and studied the older woman's face. "Thank you... for everything. I spent my whole life wondering about you... if I looked like you. I've never looked like anyone before... it's the darndest thing."

She stared into her mother's eyes and she welled up again. "I have your eyes...oh Mom...I needed you so many times." Kathleen held Laura's face in her hands. "I've always loved you...more than anything or anyone in this world. I dreamed a thousand times that I held you in my arms...but now... you must go. You simply must." Laura fixed herself and wiped her eyes. "I know."

They walked to the door and hugged one more time. Kathleen watched Laura as she sat into the car and drove out of her life. She closed the door and collapsed to her knees in abject grief.

CHAPTER EIGHT: AS GOD INTENDED

'I learned that courage was not the absence of fear, but the triumph over it.'
Nelson Mandela - Political Leader

The bar was more comfortable than she'd imagined. She'd passed by it every night and often wondered what the attraction was but, now that she was here, it seemed like the kind of place she might enjoy if circumstances were different. Jim Casey collected three double whiskies from the counter. He drank one on route to the table and placed the other two in between them. Connemara Peat, Single Malt... 'The divine irrigation' as Jim described it. The bar was filling up and the mutterings got louder so he speaks up "I'm really sorry about your mother. She paid a terrible price, poor woman... I suppose they all did."

Laura sighed deeply and ran her fingers through her hair. "It's just so... fucked up... if you'll pardon my French." He held his hand up as he took a gulp. "I've heard the word before... and it wasn't in French I can tell you. How do you feel about going home?" She sipped on her whiskey and drifted deep into thought.

He thought she'd missed the question but by the time he went to repeat it, she sat up and replied. "Strangest thing happened today. I was in Limerick and..." She drifted back into thought for a moment before continuing "...I was

DELPHINE

in Limerick and, for a moment, I could have been in Burlington.

Just another grey place filled with strangers... just another place to pass through on the way to somewhere else. But there are things I've gotten attached to here..."She turned to him "...people." He was quick to respond. "You're also in danger... and those who care about you deeply... me included... would rather suffer on without you than watch you suffer on... if that makes sense." She nodded and swirled her glass.

She rested against him with her head on his shoulder and she stared at the table when she spoke "I really am going to miss you..." He leaned down to look into her face. "You can always have me over for a holiday. I can bang a bodhrán at one of your book launches." She slapped his arm playfully.
"Stop. Anyway you wouldn't like most of those people... assholes sipping wine and talking about the book they'll never finish. There's a lot to like here... an honesty."

He finished his drink and stood up to get another. "Yes and the devil is out on Kilchoman Road so you need to get as far away from here as your royalties will take you. Be back in a minute." He walked toward the bar as several traditional Irish musicians enter.

1970: Time had changed little. The furniture was new but the bunt orange sofa and floral carpet were merely the upgrades of a familiar scene. A timber block was burning in the fire hearth and a turntable had replaced the gramophone on the same wooden stand. Eileen Brady was sitting at one end of the sofa with a single suitcase on the floor beside her. She looked vacant. Kathleen Brady was on a matching armchair by the fire and her suitcase was in front, by her knees. She seemed anxious. Both women were in their mid-30's now and two young girls, 2 or 3years of age, were playing with a music box by the fire. The door opened and Anna Brady shuffled in. She was old and feeble as she made her way slowly across the room.

Kathleen stood up to meet her. Anna embraced her and she kissed her warmly. "My sweet Kathleen..." and then to Eileen who was still staring vacantly from the sofa. "My lovely Eileen... two sides of an old woman's heart."

Kathleen spoke in hushed tones. "Come with us... please." Anna was grieving but she stayed strong. "I must stay... to make sure he never finds you... or the girls". The moment was lost on Eileen. She stared past them and a constant tremble ran through her body. Her hands shook and her head quivered as if a terrible frost has consumed her. Anna stroked her hair but Eileen did not respond. Kathleen sat by her sister. "I'll take care of her but I can't let him do the same thing to Laura and Marie. They deserve to live like children... to enjoy the fun of a fair... to know that innocence... so this stops now." Anna went to a drawer and removed a Polaroid camera. She turned and took a moment to look at them all. Her smile was steeped in sadness. "One last time...for the album." She took the final photo and there was a faint buzz as the picture appeared. The image became clear and, as it did, Anna was overcome with grief and steadied herself on the arm of an empty armchair. Kathleen rushed to her and eased her onto the seat. She was tending to her when the melody of the music box tinkled about the room and Eileen spoke softly in the background. "No... don't do that..." Kathleen responded without looking. "She's not well Eileen... I need your help." But Eileen did not help. She spoke again and her voice was fragile. "No... don't do that...Daddy."

Kathleen turned around and found Eileen lumbering toward an open front door. Laura was sitting alone by the fire and Marie was gone. Kathleen came running from the house pulling Eileen behind her. She looked left and right but Marie was nowhere to be seen. She rushed to the side of the house with Eileen in tow and both women were shocked by the sight that greeted them.

Edward Brady was walking toward the lake. He was holding Marie's hand as she stumbled along innocently beside him. He had his back to them as they called out but, although age had been brutal, he trudged forward regardless. Kathleen was running at pace and Eileen cried out as she followed close behind. Edward reached the edge of the lake and he took Marie in his arms. He stepped into the water and waded deeper in.

Kathleen was screaming as Eileen wailed pitifully. They reached the lake as Edward lowered the child into the water. She kicked and clawed at him but he held her under with a steel grip. He glared at the women with utter disdain and, as Kathleen reached them, he threw an arm out and knocked her back. The kicking stopped and the lake went quiet.

Some time had passed and the bar had gotten busy. The musicians were in full swing and Jim Casey was belting out a tune on a fiddle. Laura watched him through the crowd and he winked to her as the bar clapped along. The piece came to a finish and there was generous applause. He handed the fiddle back and went to join her. Laura was upbeat. "You didn't have to stop playing. I was enjoying that." He sat beside her and the mood was momentarily lightened. "It's my party piece... they expect it of me. Later they'll expect me to shake my fist and call them all arseholes but I'll have to disappoint them. Will I see you tomorrow?" She went quiet and sipped from her drink. "I don't think either of us are the tearful goodbye types. Let's just say our farewells tonight... drunk as God intended." They raised their glasses and clinked a toast to themselves.

When the bar was closed and the night was over, they walked to the hotel lobby. She watched him as he ambled toward the door and she smiled as he turned to face her. "You sure you're gonna be okay in that lift. They can be complicated." She took off her boots and picked them up. She stepped back barefoot. "Are you suggesting I take you to my room? I've only got one bed so... I'm not really sure how that works" He swayed over toward her. "That would make me cheap... a tart." She looked him up and down. "I could eat a tart right now... even a cheap one."

DELPHINE

The kissed as they entered the bedroom and the lights were left off. They undressed each other in the dark and they moved in unison as they reached the bed. The moonlight allowed just enough clarity for him to see her face on the pillow and she was as beautiful to him as every aria and every landscape and every verse he'd ever known. He ran his fingers along the contours of her face and along her neck and her body was so wonderfully honest. He whispered to her in the dark "It's been a while... and I'm not entirely sure this thing works." and he reassured her "...but I'll give it my best for about thirty seconds... if God spares me that long." They laughed and, beyond their window, the world was oblivious.

The room was in darkness and they slept in total silence. She had her arm across him but she shifted away and he moved in another direction. They rested back into it. Her breathing was heavy. There was the sound of a latch clicking and the door of a built in wardrobe creaked open. Laura's breath turned icy cold. A dark figure emerged from behind the wardrobe door and turned to face them. They did not wake and the silence was absolute. The figure began to glide slowly forward. Her breath was now a freezing vapour. The figure stopped beside her pillow. It raised a pale, decayed hand and reached out to touch her face. As the skeletal fingers made contact, Laura opened her eyes and sat up.

The room was empty with the exception of Jim Casey snoring on the far side of the bed. She laid back down and was shocked to find a third party in the bed with them. Edward Brady laid between them and, as Laura turned to look, he turned toward her at the same time so that her face was mere inches from his. He smiled and raised his hands to her face where she witnessed a still beating foetus curled up in his palms. It cried out. She jumped from the bed and ran screaming from the room. She staggered and fell as Edward appeared through the doorway.

The first bank of lights went out as he glided toward her in the dark. She got up and sprinted toward the light. As he got closer, more lights faded out. He was at the edge of darkness reaching out now...just inches from her. She sprinted for the last of the light. As she turned a corner, he was touching the collar of her nightdress but he came to sudden stop. Up ahead, two figures draped in black stood silently in the hallway.

Laura fell to the ground as Edward Brady reeled backward and the figures rushed forward. He retreated and, as he did the lights came alive. Up ahead, Jim Casey was standing naked away from the bedroom door. Edward Brady came snarling toward him with the shrouded figures in pursuit as Jim turned and sprinted, bare arsed, up the hall and disappeared inside the doorway. The figures chased Brady until the darkness was gone and so were they. The hallway fell silent as Jim reappeared with a duvet that he draped around Laura and they staggered back inside.

DELPHINE

In the morning light, Jim woke to find Laura gone. He went to the wardrobe and discovered all her clothes missing. He found the same with the dresser drawers. She was gone and he had lost her while sleeping off the trauma of the night before. He went to the window and stared outside. The rental car was still parked in its spot so he hoped she hadn't booked out yet. He got dressed and rushed into the lobby. The receptionist directed him to the garden at the back of the hotel and it was here, on a wooden swing seat, that he found her. She looked worn down and she barely acknowledged him as he approached. He sat beside her and they swung in silence for a while. She didn't turn to him when she spoke and her voice was so filled with desperation that it hurt him to hear it. "What am I to do now? He'll find me... and one of these nights... he'll take me away and I'll be hell bound... like those children trapped in the house." She turned to him now and she was matter of fact. "You must never contact me... don't even think of me... he'll hear your thoughts and come for you too." She stroked his face and she watched him and he stood silently and left.

The afternoon arrived and she finally got up. She collected her suitcase and stowed it in the back seat of her rental. She drove to the airport and handed the car back before going inside and checking her flight details. Flight EI380 to London, Heathrow and Air Canada flight AC857 to Pearson International, Toronto. She was about to join the queue for the book-in desk, when she felt a hand on her luggage and it was taken from her. She turned and was surprised to find Jim Casey holding both her case and one of his own. She was totally confused but, he but the bags down and embraced her. She reacted angrily and shook him off. "Didn't you listen to a word I said? You need to get as far away from me as possible. I'm catching a flight back home and I'll take my chances with Delphine." Jim nodded. "I heard you. I've heard every word you said since you got here and you're correct about one thing. You're catching a flight alright but not to Toronto." He took two tickets from inside his jacket. "In just under two hours' time, we're going to Ataturk airport in Istanbul and, from there, we're flying to Çanakkale. We're going to find Hassan Yildrim and Yusuf Alpman and Umut Batuk and we're going to stand at the gates of hell together because I won't live the rest of my life not knowing if you're okay." She sighed and reached for her luggage. "This is not your fight Jim." But he tightened his grip and spoke through his anger. "That son of a bitch almost knocked me over without as much as a pair of socks on me... and I pick my own fights. My father was afraid of Edward Brady... but I'm not my father." He took the bags and started toward the British Airways desk. She walked slowly at first but, when she caught up with him, they moved with purpose.

DELPHINE

CHAPTER NINE: THE LAST WALTZ

'Who controls the past, controls the future. Who controls the present, controls the past.'
George Orwell - English Author

The stopover in Istanbul facilitated a decent meal and the opportunity to freshen up. The morning had been such a scramble and the only thing on Laura's mind had been to flee post-haste. She was in Turkey but that could just as easily have been Toronto or even Timbuktu had the Canadian flight been fully booked. It wasn't Drumasheen and that was their only focus after the late night events in the hotel. The trip out was largely a silent one and, other Laura voicing her concerns about Jim getting so involved, they took the opportunity to sleep and catch up on some much needed rest.

Çanakkale was a surprise package in several respects.
Firstly, it was a truly stunning city and, as they drove toward the hotel, the coastal view with its setting sun, was straight from a 'wish you were here'. Secondly, for a city that had seen real investment, it was still incredibly proud of its ties to the old world and one could easily see its links to a layer of centuries. The Hotel Athena was warm and welcoming and their room was clean and comfortable. They slept the sleep of the dead and, for that night at least, they were undisturbed.

DELPHINE

The morning came far too quickly and, following a light breakfast, they walked along the beach on their way to the city. They were halted by the sight of a Trojan horse and took a few minutes to investigate but they were here on a quest and nothing else mattered more than that. They arrived in the city and followed a map until they came to an old stone street called Assos. It meandered downhill like a snake and the cobblestone avenue was lined with churches and bazaars. Assos fed into several side streets and, on the corner of one such street, they came upon a very curious shop indeed. This was öbür dünya and it was not what they'd expected when it was described as an antiquities specialists.

The store itself was an antique with its array of pots and pans that were hooked from a wooden window cover. The front window was decorated with farmyard rakes, kerosene lamps, pitchers and urns and a very dried and cracked leather suitcase. They went inside.

The items on display inside the store were of better quality than those that lined the window. Several golden pots could be seen along with a variety of well stained glass pieces and Jim noted several 18th and 19th century firearms mounted on the walls. As they neared the counter, a Turkish woman in her 60's appeared from a back room and greeted them with a smile. She wore a traditional embroidered kaftan with an ornamental golden headdress and she opened her two palms skyward as she curtsied. Laura was the first to speak. She looked around and said "Very beautiful." Then she spoke slowly and clearly. "We are looking for Hassan... Hassan Yildrim." The Turkish lady stared from Laura to Jim and back to Laura again. The hospitality slipped and she answered in curt tones. "No Hassan here. Now thank you." There was a movement in the back room and they could hear a chair dragging on a stone floor. The Turkish lady became irate and started ushering them from the shop. "Go now... thank you. No Hassan. You no come again... thank you." Laura protested but they were out on the street and the door was locked behind them.

As the evening fell, Laura and Jim had made their way back to Assos Street and they sat outside a tea room where they could still see the shop front of öbür dünya. At just after 6pm, they witnessed the Turkish lady emerge from the store in jeans and a jacket with Nike runners and a denim shoulder bag. She held the door wide open and they watched as a hunched old man in a brown suit and black Kufi prayer cap shuffled into the street with her assistance. She linked the old man's arm and they heard her refer to him as 'Baba' which means father. Laura and Jim did not waste time. They were upon them in seconds and confusion made way for anger as the lady protested in Turkish and they called out 'Hassan' to the bewildered old man who had little or no idea what was happening. Voices were raised and arms waved until everything was brought to silence by the chimes of a music box from inside Laura's bag.

Laura reached into her bag and brought the box into the open. The lid was open and Delphine danced for all to see. The old man became stunned and stared at the box with eyes as wide as saucers. He reached out to touch it but stopped inches short and pulled his hand away. His daughter shed bitter tears as he removed his kufi cap and prayed intensely to his God. When he was finished he looked to them and spoke. "I was told... someone would come...one day... but that... was many years ago." Laura closed the box.

"My mother came looking for Hassan a very long time ago... but she was told by a young lady that no one knew of you. You are Hassan right?" He nodded and whispered to his daughter. "This was you?" She wiped her eyes and nodded.

"These are dark forces... and I did not want you getting hurt
Baba." He rested his hand on her and spoke softly "Birtanem...benim çocuğum." He turned to Laura and pointed at the box. "May I?" She gave it to him and he closed his eyes as he held it firmly in both hands. He prayed quietly before opening his eyes and handing it back. "We have much to do" He said.

Laura was asleep in her bedroom armchair when a figure walked by and the lights flickered. She woke just as the figure walked out into the hotel hallway and she walked past the sleeping Jim Casey to the opened door where she stared outside. A man in a dark suit was walking away from the apartment and she felt a compulsion to follow him. He turned a bend and, when she caught up, she noticed that his shoes were missing and he was walking barefoot. She stayed close as he turned onto another hallway and, when she turned with him, she discovered that his jacket and shirt were missing and he was naked from the waist up.

Each time that she walked faster, the figure just seemed farther away so she kept pace with it. On the next turn, the figure was entirely naked but she noticed a trickle of blood streaming from its buttocks and, as the figure walked onto the next hallway, it was as if an invisible whip was lashing down. He winced under the pain and lacerations cut deep into his flesh. There was blood daubed along the clear white walls as he fell to the ground and she was upon him. He turned over and pleaded as he poured out and Laura was shocked and distraught to find that it was Shane Kelly.

It was as if all the air had been sucked out and, when he opened his mouth to scream, he was frozen in his silent torment. She woke with a start to find the room empty and, after she'd found her bearings, she climbed into the bed where she wrapped an arm around Casey.

They shared breakfast with Hassan in the hotel lobby and they sat with their luggage waiting for transport to take them on the next leg of the journey. He told them that they would go to Bigali where Yusuf Alpman would make arrangements to take them into the mountains. Hassan warned them gravely that dangers lay ahead and that the eyes of the beast would not be far as they got closer. Laura had sensed the presence and she'd felt that her dream encounter with Kelly was a genuine foreboding. She'd phoned The Burren Arms earlier to be told that the manager was still missing, that staff members had called to his empty apartment and that a report had been filed with the local police station. She worried for him but there were matters to be dealt with here before she could lend her hand in Clare. A pick-up truck pulled into the bay outside the hotel and they climbed aboard.

The drive to Bigali should have taken less than an hour but somewhere in the region of Behramli, the vehicle went off road and started toward the wooded hills above them. This brought Laura and Jim to a sombre silence as it seemed an entirely impromptu detour and their anxiety escalated when the pick-up stopped and three heavily robed and armed men climbed in back. They shouted orders in Turkish and the driver obeyed. They stayed mountainside for the duration and it appeared they were hiding in the pine arches. Once Bigali was in sight, they made a quick descent and the armed men disembarked at the very outskirts of the village.

Bigali was a hamlet trapped in time. The buildings hadn't aged a day since WW1 and the streets were a capsule called 1918. Turkish flags were on liberal display and images of Mustafa Kemal Ataturk were either painted on the building exteriors or hung from flags draped across the town square. Old men sipped Turkish tea outside long forgotten cafes and the women sorted leather goods on rickety tables in the market area. It wasn't until they wandered inside a building and found glass cases of photos and document, that Laura and Jim realized that Bigali was a museum town, a perfectly preserved representation of life in the Great War. It fascinated her that it was here, in this very patch, that Edward and his comrades had come for supplies and it was on these very roads that he had encountered the child with Delphine. It reminded her of why they were there and that brought a sense of dread that she might have forgotten in the sun and the soft air.

The driver brought them to a market cafe and told them to wait until a contact arrived. They ordered Mahmood tea and baklava and they were pleasantly surprised when generous helpings arrived. As they settled in, Laura seemed unusually anxious and Jim picked up on it. She'd been on edge for some time and he'd noticed her staring at him when they cutting through the mountains in the pick-up. He spoke as he stirred his tea "You okay? Tell the truth, it's the smell... the least they could have done was install a shower in the truck." She seemed genuinely nervous but, as he went to speak again, she cut across him. "I have something to tell you...something that could change the way you view me." He wanted to lighten the moment but he couldn't disrespect it in that way. "Some years ago" she continued "I found myself... unhappily pregnant." She buried her face down low. "I was not ready... no... I was never ready to be a mother and the thought terrified me more than anything in this life."

Her head was still bowed. "I couldn't have something relying so heavily on me... not when I couldn't rely on myself. It wasn't something I could just forget about. I felt that it was feeding off me every second of every hour and I couldn't run in any direction to make it better... and I panicked... and I had an abortion." She exhaled and her entire body slumped. "There I said it... Jesus... you've no idea how difficult that was." She waved air into her face with both hands and took a deep breath. She stared at him. "It haunts me, you see, and it's haunted me since I arrived in Drumasheen."

He thought before answering. "That's understandable. You can't go digging around in your past and not expect to leave that bare." He laid a hand on hers. "Are you okay Laura?" She considered the question and scanned his face with a great intensity before replying. "The question is... are you okay? I've lived with this for many years."

He sat back and sighed. "There's a scene in the movie Jaws where Robert Shaw and Richard Dreyfuss start comparing scars and they try to outdo each other with the biggest wound." He raises one hand to represent Dreyfuss "Teeth marks on his arm... Moray eel." Then he raised the other arm to represent Shaw. "Knuckle damage to his head... St Paddy's Day...Boston." He is filled with a raw empathy as he continues. "We could start trading scars, you and I, but the past is the past." He holds her hands in his. "What we did yesterday does not define who we are today... not when the biggest mountain we'll ever climb is simply learning to live with our regrets. You must never lose your compassion for someone who was so very lost in the world... even if that person was you." He stood and walked to the counter and ordered more tea and baklava.

Shortly before 5pm, a Turkish soldier arrived to the cafe in search of them. They found him immediately intimidating and left with him very reluctantly. He was in his 50's, with a stocky build and he sported a very well developed moustache so that he bore a resemblance to Saddam Hussein. He was curt with them and practically ordered them into a military jeep. They felt in grave danger and, when the jeep went off road, Jim attempted to speak with him but there was no response. Night fell and the lights of the jeep illuminated nothing more than dirt road and wild gorse for mile after mile. Eventually they saw lights in the darkness and a small group of buildings came into view. The jeep stopped and they got out. As they walked toward the buildings, Jim watched the soldier take out his sidearm and turn. He stared blankly and they stared back in dread. He raised the gun and instinctively Jim stepped across to cover Laura. Two shots rang out and they looked behind them to see a very large and very dead Armenian viper still coiled a few feet behind them. It had been almost upon them and they simply hadn't known. The soldier beckoned them forward and they followed more willingly. They stopped outside a building and the soldier went inside.

Shortly after, he re-emerged with an older man who was dressed entirely in black including his taqiyah turban. He was a sombre looking individual who spoke to his own people with an air of authority. He eyed them from a distance and he spoke to those around him without taking his eyes off Laura and Jim. Then he approached them and asked to see the music box. Laura handed it over and, after inspecting the piece thoroughly, he asked them to follow him as he toward a well-lit building on the compound. They were brought to a sparsely furnished room and told to sit while a bed was lifted from another room and brought to rest in front of them. A very frail and weathered old lady sat, propped up in the bed.

The soldier stepped forward and spoke in surprisingly good English. He introduced himself as Alda Alpman an officer of Türk Kara Kuvvetleri, the Turkish Land Forces. The gentleman in the black robes was his father, Yusuf Alpman and the lady in the bed was the most revered and cherished child of God, Umut Batuk. He said that the destined paths of each of their lives were present at that very moment and he said he would allow Umut to explain with his translation. She was raised up further in the bed and it became apparent to Laura and Jim that she was hopelessly blind.

Umut asked for the box and it was given to her. She ran her hands over it to great delight and, when she opened it and the chimes played, she laughed and cried with equal vigour. When the tune finished, she closed the box and called for Alda Alpman to translate. She whispered to him but he spoke loudly and clearly. She said that, unlike her, her Grandfather was a seer and, long before the Great War, he had foreseen the breach of the fortress, the desecration of the sarcophagus and he had seen the tragedy that befell the young Irish soldier at Gallipoli.

He knew what would follow so he procured a music box and had his daughter sit by the roadside in advance of the soldiers march all those years ago. But, in order for the conjuring to work, they would require some private possession of his, something so intimate and personal that both his heart and soul were invested in it. When the child saw the carving, she asked him what it was and he whispered that it was 'The Last Waltz' between him and his wife before he left for war. The box was exchanged for it and a ritual was held so that the box could become the armoury for his displaced soul.

The old lady called for a satchel and it was given to her. She reached inside and removed the wood carving. She continued and Alpman in turn translated. The child on the roadside was her mother and, ever since that moment, it was expected that someday, someone would come seeking redemption. Her grandfather and her mother had died waiting and she had grown old and frail in the company of Yusuf Alpman who had cared for her needs both spiritual and physical. Their lives had been dedicated to a final confrontation with the Iblis and that time was now upon them. She said that the Iblis might be forced to the netherworld but it could not be killed.

She said that it had been contained with the nail of Helena which penetrated the right hand of the true God. Helena, mother of the Emperor Constantine, had taken the relic from Jerusalem in 315 AD and it was venerated by the first Council of Nicaea. The Lords of darkness and light then used the nail to entomb the creature and they would need to identify it.

When Jim asked what that meant, he was told they would have known the demons heart and that, if they did, they would know what had to be done. The old lady spoke continuously and Alda Alpman translated. Umut said that the demon had been bound by the power of two talismans, one containing the vile blood of Bael and the other holding the blessed blood of Emmanuel. The blood of Bael had been stolen when the sarcophagus was desecrated and the soldier who took it had died on the Somme. The talisman he carried had been lost there in the mud and the madness it had created. She said that only the Amulet of Emmanuel weighed the demon down now and they would be allowed no more than one drop of its blessed content so they would have to be extremely careful.

She said that the blood should flow along Helena's nail and that it should be driven into the heart of the beast. She finished by thanking God for allowing her to complete her mission and, in conclusion of her duties, she handed 'The
Last Waltz' carving to Laura. Alda Alpman then asked Laura and Jim to leave. He said that Umut Batuk would now tell his father the exact location of the fortress and that he would take them there the following evening. The morning would be reserved for prayer and meditation so he had an assistant place them in separate rooms for the night.

Sleep did not come easy for either of them but, when Jim attempted to access her room in the early hours, he found an armed guard in place. He wanted to make sure she was okay as it had been a particularly rough day on her but he had come to admire her greatly and he knew her heart was strong. He looked across at the empty side of his bed and found that he really missed her. Had someone told him a week ago that he would re-open his heart to someone, he would have laughed and downed a double. Now here he was, miles from everything he knew, everything he was comfortable with and everything he could hide behind. Tomorrow he would face hell in the literal sense and, that he would do it with her and for her, was all that mattered to him.

She stared through a window at the night sky and wondered if she might ever see it as clearly again. It dazzled with a billion flickering lights and she thought it might have resembled the cave of Ali Baba. But that was just a moral tale and the cave they would encounter tomorrow would not open and shut on command. They had no idea what lay in the depths of that lair and she felt truly conflicted that Jim was descending that spiral with her. She remembered him trying to protect her when Alda Alpman shot the viper and she knew he believed it was sacrifice at the time. She felt that she didn't deserve him and, now that he knew about her past, perhaps he'd start to feel the same way. Her guilt was overwhelming at times but now that she was righting the wrongs of the past with the Iblis then maybe, just maybe, she could lump her own wrongs into that melting pot.

The morning started off with a startling revelation and, if the rest of the day was to follow suit, then they might be advised just fly home now. They met in the market area by their building and stopped into the tea room for some breakfast. As Jim poured, they heard the wailing of a funeral procession and they could see the cortege make its way along the stone avenue behind a coffin that was hoisted shoulder high. As they came past, Laura and Jim were stunned to see

Yusuf and Alda Alpman holding up a banner with the image of Umut Batuk. She was as good as her word and she had found freedom on the completion of her own duties. Death and loss were the cornerstones of this entire saga and they hung their heads in reverent prayer that success in their endeavours would see a change in that fate. They joined in with the cortege and were taken toward a small, whitewashed church nearby.

The day was a time for reflection and they spent much of it alone and apart. The women dressed Laura in white and she was encouraged to pray to whatever God she was familiar with. The others prayed that her words would be heard and her soul would be cleansed so that, should she die later that evening, she would face the lord in presentable fashion. Jim was taken by Yusuf Alpman and several of the old men. They drank tea and offered him their hookahs so that they might make a bond and that treaty that would go with him into the depths as they would pray outside. The sun shone down on all of them and the villagers rejoiced that Umut Batuk now rested in the warmth of heaven.

Evening arrived and nerves began to set in. Jim sucked on the hookah like it was a dying man's last request. He began pacing shortly after 3pm and now at 5.15pm, he'd worn his sandals out. Laura sat in absolute silence since noon. She contemplated life past, present and future and she tried to keep her breathing in check but there was a waver on it now, a quiver that stunted her breath into minor instalments. At 5.30pm, Yusuf called for them and they appeared into the market where the local population had gathered. People shook their hand as they passed and a few offered blessings. They were loaded into the jeep and they set off into the night.

They drove for an hour and the terrain was particularly rough. The mountainside had no road other than a pathway and they bobbled along peaks and divots until they began to see a steeper face to the summit. The jeep went as far as it could and they began to walk by burning torchlight. Yusuf and Aldo kept a vigilant guard and the carried their rifles cocked and ready. A mist had gathered around the base of the summit and they waded through it. They looked up ahead and they could see great clumps of wild-growth and Yew trees that centred in one area and, at this point, the Alpmans stopped. Aldo explained that it was forbidden to enter and that Laura and Jim would have to go alone from here. They trudged ahead and stumbled through briar and thorn before breaching the green shield and standing at the mouth of Hell.

Jim held his torch forward and he led the way while Laura held hers behind and checked the path behind them as they inched forward. After a while, they came to a stone stairs cut into the mountain and it spiralled down exactly as Edward had depicted in his letters. The watched their footing as the ground beneath them became unsteady and each foot forward yielded a crunching sound. They stopped and held their torches knee high. Thousands of insects milled around by their feet and giant centipedes undulated over their sandals as another world of arachnids scurried along the stone walls. They picked up pace and descended into the lair as quickly as their fear would allow.

Once they reached the bottom, Jim saw some torch holders with the remnants of candles and he proceeded to light what could be lit. The area came into view and they were both left in silence at the sight of a 9ft sarcophagus mounted on a stone slab altar. They gathered together and gave it everything to remove the lid. One great push and it crashed to the floor.

They stared at each other before looking inside, the job had to be done so they turned on it together. The creature inside was inhuman. It was monstrous in its proportions and it looked utterly demonic and decidedly other worldly. The eye sockets were huge and oval, with the head disproportionately large for the body. The arms were unusually long but the cadaver had a muzzle and teeth that were intended to tear and rip. As they leaned in, the flame from their torches danced against the rich red pendant that the creature wore about its neck. It lay on its chest as if it were weighed down by it. Laura lifted it slowly and, as she did, Jim became aware of the half inch wide hole in the creatures chest. "You must know what's in its heart" said Jim in reference to Umut Batuk. He closed his fist and brought it down so that it broke through and he was inside the sternum.

He reached around in absolute disgust and, when he pulled his fist back out, there was a 7 inch crucifixion nail concealed in his claw. He held it to the torchlight and he gasped. The leathery remains of a heart wall clung to the rusted iron and he peeled it away to reveal the entire relic. Jim could not contain his awe "Christ on a cross." Laura took it from him and she placed her open shoulder bag on the sarcophagus. She removed the amulet from the beast and opened it at one end.

She tipped it over against the iron tip of Helena's nail and the thick viscous liquid formed a bubble, a solitary drop of divine blood that pooled and fell. She looked into the bag and the drop had landed on the carved hands of the waltzing couple as they reached for heaven. Laura took the moment to ask that Edward and Anna be together again and she covered the tip of the nail before placing it in her bag. They were about to leave when the whispering started. It was faint at first but it got stronger and there were many sources.

They held their torches aloft and edged forward. There were other sounds now, hissing and snarling. It was as if the volume had been turned to max and they chamber was a symphony of sinister sounds. As the light illuminated beyond them, they could see vipers and asps that slithered forth and, on the stairwell, a pack of grey wolves snarled and gnashed their teeth as they descended upon Laura and Jim. But it was the shadows that terrified most of all. Black shapes that darted along the cold stone and reached out to take them.

Undulating masses that closed in on them with such dark intent that they oozed pitch black from their empty sockets. They were surrounded and, as they waved their torches and bought precious seconds, they knew the end was surely in sight.

The asps slid closer, the wolves bared their teeth and, as arachnids dropped upon them, the shadows darted forward and totally engulfed Jim. He was taken to the floor and he was dragged into the dark. Laura could hear the pack rip in as Casey cried out and, as she went to help, the shadows cornered her too. They rose up along the length of her body and she could feel their cold embrace as they tightened around her thighs and her breasts and her throat and the life was being sucked from her with each exhale. All was lost.

The mission had failed and a century of suffering would have been in vain. Laura closed her eyes and waited.

Suddenly there was a squeal from the pack and a huge hiss from the vipers nest as a bright light illuminated the entire chamber sending every living and near-dead thing scurrying.

Laura was barely able to look upon it and Jim Casey, bitten and bloody, picked up his torch and staggered to her.

Together they shuffled past the explosive light and, as they did, Laura looked deep into the glow and saw a figure at its source. She raised a hand over her eyes to dim the glare and she was both shocked and saddened as the image of Shane Kelly became clear as the radiance about him pulsated with a raw power. She felt an overwhelming sorrow and reached out to touch him. "Shane... have you passed over?"

His voice was soft. "I'm in the half-light now sister. I won't be able to help you next time we meet... and you can't save me... no one can... so... go now!"

They climbed the stairs at speed and they burst out into the night to the joy and jubilation of Yusuf and Aldo Alpman. She tended to Jim's wounds that night and they slept together in silence until mornings light rushed through their window. She woke with her face pressed to his chest and he kissed her forehead as they stretched. This part of the journey was over and they would never see Bigali or Çanakkale or Seytanın Beşiği again... or maybe they would... life is what happens when you're making other plans. But they paid reverence to the memory of Umut Batuk and started the long journey toward home.

DELPHINE

CHAPTER TEN: A FAMILY REUNION

'There ain't no difference, they both feel exactly the same on the inside, they both fear dyin' and gettin 'hurt. It's what the hero does that makes them a hero and what the other doesn't do that makes them a coward.'
Cus D'Amato – Boxing Trainer

They did not go directly home. As they drove toward Drumasheen, a decision was taken that, sometimes, retreat is the best form of attack and they would regroup in the confines of Connemara. They drove past the Ennis slip-road, through Galway City, past the lakes of Oughterard and The Quiet Man Bridge, up by Maam Cross and into the beating heart of the West, Clifden. If there had been a bridge from there to Greenland and enough diesel in the tank, they would have taken it in turns to drive. But they were about as far as they needed to go and, following a hot chowder with freshly baked mini loaves, they settled into a bar where local musicians tapped a rhythm to their patrons applause and the world sat on the other side of the Connemara Hills.

It was a million miles from Bigali and, now that they were surrounded by stout and singers, the past few days seemed like a dream to them... a very vivid and terrifying dream. But, of course, it wasn't and, each time he saw the angst etched onto her face, he reached for her hand and sang a little louder. There was an overwhelming feeling that, one way or another, they were drifting toward a dark and unpredictable fate and all they knew was that the climax would involve a confrontation like none they'd ever experienced. They were scared and it was just that simple.

Laura had weighed up the options and, fragile as the human condition was, she had considered simply running but all roads must end and, eventually, so would hers. She had seen the commitments made by Umut and Yusuf, the tragedies endured by Anna and the neglect and abuse suffered by Kathleen and Eileen. Would she just end up as another name on that list, another atrocity on the account of Edward Brady... the abomination.

That night they sat silent and thought deep. They both knew that questions would come long before they breached the Connemara Hills and, whenever they came, it would be time enough. This was going to be a live event with no dress rehearsal and, ultimately, the answers would be dissected only in the aftermath if, indeed, that outcome allowed for an aftermath. Nothing would ever be the same again once this was over and they were reminded of the line in the Harry Chapin song W.O.L.D *'You can travel all of ten thousand miles and still stay where you are.'* So they decided to simply get out of their heads as a means of escapism and they drank and danced like the party would roll forever. In the end, they carried each other upright and, when sleep took charge of them, it was a job entirely well done.

The following morning was slow but wasn't a standstill. There was an understanding that this was, most probably, the last full day, so they hit the shower early, had as much of a breakfast as they could hold down and packed everything into her airport rental. There was a sharp air that day and it cut through some of the excess from the night before. As they pulled away from the car park, they felt a little like outlaws on the run, like Bonnie Parker & Clyde Barrow only older and less wanted. They embarked on the Connemara Loop but started at the Benedictine Monastery, Kylemore Abbey. They drank coffees and sat on the opposite side of the river so that the Abbey looked like a wing of Helms Deep awaiting the armies of Saruman and the ire of Sauron himself. The time for staying ahead of the pack was over and the questions should be asked now before they pointed the car hood toward Clare.

He took the lead and broke the silence. "What will you do... when this is over?" he asked. She sipped her coffee.
"That depends." He pushed a little harder. "Do you think you might ever see yourself here... even from time to time?" She raised her eyes to his and smiled just a little. "That depends." He nodded and continued. "So... when do we do this or how do we do this?" The sarcasm crept back in "Let's face it, this could be like a first class ticket on the Kursk." She put her coffee down. "You could have said Titanic... at least we'd go down in style." She thought and spoke again. "I suspect we 'have to go looking for him. Once we get there... he'll be waiting. Jim?" He was surprised to see her trembling. "Jim... I'm so fucking scared! If this doesn't work... for whatever reason, he'll... have me... and I'll be like Anna." The chill cut just a bit

deeper and he put his jacket over her shoulders. He hugged her as they walked back to the car. "I won't let that happen." he said "and we'll hit the bastard together... like Butch and Sundance... or Thelma and Louise... hell hath no fury like Susan Sarandon in size 12 stilettos!" She rested her head against his shoulder as they walked to the car and the first drizzle of rain sprayed upon them.

The loop was not without its high points and they drove through the rain from Rinvyle along the wild coast to
Glassillaun across the great lakes to Derrynassliggaun and into Leenaun where they left the motorway and took the rugged road through the bleak and beautiful isolation of Maum and, once more, into Maam Cross. From here it was a drive into darkness as the winter was unforgiving and the rain lashed their car as if to push them back. But, as the Clare border eventually loomed large, she voiced her concern. "Thelma and Louise... they drove off a cliff you know... doesn't sound very promising." He sighed deeply. "I should have gone for Laurel and Hardy but I didn't want you feeling paranoid about your moustache." She smiled at him mockingly.

On their return to Drumasheen, Laura and Jim could have been forgiven for believing that life as they knew it had changed forever, that the entire village would be out with burning torches and pitchforks but, as they drove through the town at night, it appeared that business as usual was still the order of the day. They didn't stop until they came to Casey's house and, following the recent incidents at The Burren, it was decided that Laura was best off staying with Jim rather than risking a repeat performance of those events.

As he slept that night, she watched him from her pillow and she lamented his lacerations and his wounds. She recalled how understanding he had been when she revealed her secret and she remembered how he talked about the futility of comparing scars. These scars were inflicted by her, not directly but because of his involvement with her and she didn't want that. In the morning, they would get up and face the devil again. Who knew how that would go and she really didn't want Jim hurt any more than he had been. She curled up beside him and they slept.

The house lay still and, but for the ticking of a clock, time might have stopped entirely. In the distance a dog barked several times and then went silent while a figure stood in the pouring rain and viewed Jim Casey's house from the front garden. It loomed large against the night sky and the black suit could have been lost against the midnight were it not for the spatters of mud that caked the tattered jacket and trousers. The figure stepped forward and began lumbering toward the house.

She woke to the sound of panic and she sat up as Jim came through house with his hands on his head screaming "Sweet Jesus!!" The entire room had been turned upside down and she noted that a breeze blew in through an opened front door. She jumped from the bed and rifled through her luggage but her worst fears were realized. Both Delphine and the nail were missing and she imploded in the anguish. She was inconsolable and, although he did his best, her body shuddered under the crushing reality. He paced up and down. "Fuck!! Fuck!!" He hunkered down and curled his arms over his head. "We could go back... to Bigali." He stood and protested to her. "Perhaps there's another way... Yusuf might know... there has to be something we can do!!" But she got to her feet and pounded her fists on his chest. "It's over... don't you get it? He's won... and I have to run." She stopped fighting and stared at him. "I have to run Jim... I just do! I can't impose this on you... or Kathleen... or anyone else... so..." He asked her not to move for now...he pleaded with her. "Kathleen... she'll know what to do. You must stay here... do you hear me? I could be a while but, I promise, next time I see you, we'll be ready to finish this." He held both her arms and stared through her. "Can you do that... can you just wait until I get back?" She agreed and he drove off at speed.

Laura wasted no time in packing her suitcase. She grabbed clothes and photos and stuffed them into the bag. Every so often she stopped and listened. She checked her breath for vapour and watched the closet doors. Nothing. She grabbed the bag and left in a hurry. She screeched to a halt outside the cemetery gates and got out. She moved with a sense of urgency as a strong breeze carried her from behind and urged her forward. She reached the cemetery entrance and looked inside.

Her anxiety was on full show and she took a deep breath before forcing the rusted pedestrian gate open. It grated with a shrill as she passed. Laura made her way past headstones that had long since succumbed to time but they meant little to her as she moved with both speed and caution.

She glanced left and right but the cemetery was quiet and that eased her somewhat. She arrived at the foot of a grave and she stopped in silent reverence.

There was an old headstone that had been recently engraved.
The older inscriptions read:

'In Beloved Memory of Marie Brady, Beloved Daughter, Granddaughter and Angel. Died 27th March 1970. Aged 2yrs Anna Brady, Beloved Mother and Grandmother. Died 26th September 1971. Aged 74yrs.'

The more recent inscription is at the bottom and reads:

'Eileen Brady, Beloved Sister. Died 11th November 2018. Aged 82yrs'

Laura knelt by the headstone and rested her hand upon it. She closed her eyes in silent prayer.

1971: Anna Brady was slightly hunched over as she wiped a damp cloth across the kitchen table. She was badly broken and she did not try to mask it. Her eyes had long since died but her heart was strong in a way that was entirely unwelcome by her. Sleep beckoned. Eileen appeared at the kitchen doorway. She looked worn but wary and there was a nervousness in her voice. "It's quiet... since... everyone left." Anna continued wiping down the table and did not respond. Eileen continued. "I miss them... Kathleen... Laura... and..." Anna stopped cleaning and stared at Eileen. "And Marie... I know... I miss them too. They're all gone now."

Eileen bit on her thumbnail and sounded almost childlike. "Is he gone... really gone?" Anna put the cloth away and started turning out the lights. "Bastard's in the ground where he belongs."

The last of the downstairs lights went out and they helped each other up the stairs to the illumination of a bulb on the upper hallway. The house was entirely in darkness. There was a stillness that shrouded each shape and shadow. The silence was broken by a latch turning and the front door creaked open. There was a thick fog that banked by the front steps and tendrils of it crept around the arches of the open space. A dark shape appeared from beyond the mist and trudged up the steps. The swirls danced about as it shuffled forward. A muddy shoe breached the doorway and a soil-stained trousers came into view as a wheezing breath rasped on the night air.

Anna Brady was resting on her side but a troubled sleep distressed her and she was restless. The music box sat on her bedside table and, as she turned and tossed, the lid began to open but it stopped just before the mechanism kicked in and it slowly closed shut. The handle of her bedroom door turned and the faint sound was enough to rouse her. The door slowly opened and, as it did, she turned to face it. She called out quietly. "Eileen...?" A figure shuffled forward. As the moonlight caught it, the funeral suit of Edward Brady appeared into view. It was smeared in silt and sludge. Anna gasped but, rather than be fearful, she was consumed with disappointment. She whispered. "Oh no..."

He lumbered forward and came into full view by her bedside. A decayed hand reached for a pillow. Anna rested back down and folded her rosary beads on her chest. She clutched them with both hands as she whispered for the last time. "It's over."

She stared up at him as he placed the pillow on her face and his fists pushed down with a steely determination. She struggled instinctively but not forcibly. He strengthened his grip and she went silent. He drew the pillow back to reveal the death mask of Anna Brady. She was staring blankly and a tear has run from both eyes.

Laura kissed her fingertips and placed them against the headstone. There was purpose in her step as she skipped past the headstones and, once she had gone through the pedestrian gate, she broke into a run. There was the sound of an engine revving up as an airport rental screamed out of the car park and away. She was driving toward the airport and checking through her bag as she tried to watch the road. The car swerved but she continued.

Once she was beyond the town limits, she stopped with a screech and threw her head back in despair. She knew she couldn't leave without her only protection. She called out in a mix of frustration and resignation. "Delphine..." and she punched the steering wheel in fury. She phoned Jim but gets his voice-mail. She hung up and checked her watch. It was 12.15pm. She looked to the sky and found that there was hours of daylight left. She phoned Jim and again got the same voice-mail. There was a panic as she spoke. "Jim, it's me. Look... I'm sorry about taking off but I can't leave without Delphine. It's the only way I'll ever know if he's found me. My flight isn't until 7. I'm going to wait outside the house for you." She swung the car around and sped off in the direction of the Brady house.

Laura checked her watch. It was 3.10pm. She phoned Jim again. "Please pick up... please pick up." Jim's voice-mail started and she put the phone away. She walked to the front of the house and stared through a glass panel. The music box was on full display on the table and the house was bathed in sunlight. She reached for the key. The lock turned and the door fell open. She looked around outside and saw a rock. She placed it against the door to hold it open and reluctantly went inside. She ran down the hallway and grabbed the box. She turned and began to sprint back.

The door was in sight... just a few more meters. She gave it everything and, as she did, the door under the stairs popped open and an old broom handle fell out. Her feet got caught on it and she crashed to the floor. Her head walloped off the banisters on the way down and the music box went sprawling forward. She lay unconscious.

    She came too eventually but she was bleeding and concussed. Some time had passed and, beyond the open door, she could see dusk setting in. She could not stand so she tried to crawl forward. The music box slowly opened and the melody played. She heard the first footsteps on the stairs and looked up to see the shadowed figure of Edward Brady, muddied and decayed, slowly descend. He clomped onto each step, one slow thump at a time, and she could hear him as he gasped for breath in the dark. Everything was freezing over. She opened the door under the stairs and crawled inside as the last glows of dusk faded and an early winter's night took over. She could hear him on the stairs... getting closer... in the hallway now... and she could hear him dragging his way forward. Her tears were turning to icicles and her breath was an Arctic breeze. As the door began to open she reeled backwards with a great thud and, as she did, the wood panelling behind her gave way. She fell through into a hidden room and the noise outside stopped.

    She saw a light chord in the broom cupboard and she pulled on it. The bulb was dim but it faintly illuminated the secret space beneath the stairs. It took a few moments for her eyes to adjust but she could make out figures on chairs. There was total silence. She crawled closer and stopped. There were seven chairs. The remains of five girls were seated about.

DELPHINE

They were badly decomposed but dressed in a doll-like fashion. Each child had the ragged remains of old rope that still bound their ankles... a lasting reminder of their torment and humiliation. The poorly preserved remains of a man lay in a sixth chair. His head has lolled to one side but Laura could see the massive trauma to the skull. A rocking chair in the middle of the room was empty.

As her vision adjusted to the dim, she noticed a book in the middle of the floor. The cover was familiar to her. It was her novel 'The Night Before Dawn'. She opened it and discovered an inscription that read:

'To Shane, my brother in the Burren. Love always, your eternal sister, Laura.'

She stifled her cry as she placed the novel on the ground. The cold was debilitating and she struggled to move. She attempted to crawl away but, she heard the creak of the rocking chair, she looked back. Edward Brady rested as he rolled to and fro. His voice was rich and deep. "So good of you to visit. I thought you'd forgotten us." He rested a hand on the arm of the male cadaver. "Your father here had a fighting spirit... and he passed it to you... I like that." He leaned forward and she saw him in detail for the first time.

He was monstrous and vile. Rot had spread throughout his gaunt face and filthy grey tufts of hair protruded almost comically from the sides of his otherwise bald head. But it is his eyes that struck the most fear. They were cold and dull ... devoid of compassion and filled with loathing.

He reached out his raw boned fingers. "Come and give your grandfather a kiss..." She cried out and scurried into a corner. She could hear the melody of the music box in the hallway and it played faster now. The tempo was frantic. She was trembling all over and struggling for breath as she huddled in the dark. He grinned a wicked grin "Ah there she is ... just as I remembered. Always such a good child ... always ... so sweet." His lips peeled back and revealed teeth blackened by decay. He stood and shuffled into the dark. There was the sounds of dragging and he reappeared pulling a chair that was tilted back on two legs. The sound of wood clawing on concrete indicated that the chair had weight to it. Once he was at the centre of the room, Edward turned the chair around to reveal a very naked Shane Kelly bound to it.

Kelly's ankles were tied with the same rope used on the cadavers and his arms were pulled tightly behind his back. He was smeared in excrement and blood. His mouth was gagged and his eyes were painfully swollen. His body was badly bruised and, as she looked closer, she can see a series of bite marks that ran from his chest to his groin. He stared at Laura and she stared back. He tried to cry out but the gag muffled his scream. She opened her mouth but her own scream was trapped deep within her. A shudder ran through her in waves. Edward stood behind the chair and rested his hands on Kelly's shoulders. He leaned down so that his chin was almost touching the desperate man's skull and he spoke with scorn. "A brother in the Burren ... you'd think so little of family."

He stood upright and shuffled back into the dark leaving Kelly to plead with Laura through sobs and frothed gurgles. There was a movement behind him and Edward returned carrying a length of rope. He looped the rope around Kelly's neck and crossed it over at the nape. He began pulling and Kelly's body spasmed as he was throttled. He gasped for breath and his eyes bulged as the cadavers watched in silence, each face a testament to its own suffering. Kelly stared at Laura and she watched as the life drained from his bulging eyes. His head fell slowly to one side and his face became limp but twisted. Edward released his grip on the rope and pulled Kelly's head back for inspection. "So ... blissfully broken."

He turned his attention back to Laura. She was curled into a quivering ball and she peeked at him through her fingers. He stepped out from behind the chair and she can see him more clearly. "Now... about that kiss..." He removed his suit jacket and he draped it over Kelly's head. He slipped off his tattered braces and began unbuttoning his trousers. His voice had menace. "For old times sake..." She cried out and frantically crawled toward the door. He slowly ambled after her. She made it to the hallway just as the cupboard bulb blew. He stood over her and grabbed her by the hair. He started to drag her back under the stairs. The music box sounds almost deranged as Delphine pirouetted wildly.

A violent wind was whipping up and items were being scattered about the house. She stared outside and saw a car approaching at speed. The car came to a screeching stop as Jim Casey and Kathleen Brady emerged and ran toward the door. Jim called out as horror and panic consumed him. "Laura ... oh Jesus ... CHRIST!" Edward stared straight at him and bellowed. "Mine!" The front door slammed closed, sending the rock skipping across the cracked tile floor. In the darkness, Laura struggled and she fought him with everything she had. Edward leaned down and rasped. "One for Umut Batuk ..." He yanked her back and brought a closed fist crashing to the side of her head. It numbed her and, as she reeled with the force, he rasped again "...and one for The Confessor" and he struck her for a second time. She went still and he dragged her on once more.

He was about to take her through the cupboard when the front door swung wide open. For a moment, there was silence as if the storm had never existed. The figures in black emerged from the tar of night. They slipped past Jim and Kathleen but came to a stop at the doorway. The sound exploded again and Laura's eyes opened. The figures were wailing and thrashing about. Jim and Kathleen attempted to advance but a force repelled them. Jim ran to his car as Kathleen cried out. "Call to them Laura... they need your strength!" She attempted to call out but he had a hand over her mouth. Slowly he dragged her away. She fought to pull his hand away but his grip was too strong.

Suddenly, there was the roar of an engine and the headlights of Jim's car sprang to life. The beam was dulled in the hallway but, as she grappled with The Iblis, she became aware of the scar that ran the width of her wrist. It was a thoughtless, jagged incision and the scar was a reminder of hard times and dark days. She stared at it as that pain came flooding back. There was an overwhelming sensation within her now. It came from the years of isolation, from the sadness, from the self-loathing ... and from the anger. In a moment of utter rage, she bit down through his fingers and she was free for just a second. She fell forward and screamed out. "Help me!"

There was a huge gale and the drapes were blown from the figures to reveal a young Eileen and Marie in the doorway. They came screeching forward. The spectre released Laura as they set upon him. Kathleen stumbled through the door and joined them. He was clawing at them as they attempted overwhelm him but he fought back and they were no match for him. Suddenly Laura's attention was drawn to an orb that drifted through the kitchen doorway and into the hall. It went unnoticed by all but Laura and she watched it in absolute awe. It was a solitary ball of faint light that hovered above them. The orb drifted down behind Edward and the radiating image of Anna Brady rose up. She screamed out as she locked her arms around him. The battle raged on and still they could not overwhelm him. He lashed out and threw them about. Jim rushed in and pulled Laura to her feet. He wanted to carry her to safety but this was her fight too.

Laura opened her shoulder bag and removed 'The Last Waltz' carving. She could see the fingers of the figurines stained black with the blood that had dripped from Helena's Nail, the blood of Emmanuel. She grabbed the carving with both hands and ran at the beast. She plunged the blood stained point of the carving into the creatures' chest. The music box was playing but the melody was distorted. Edward cried out in a piercing scream as the Brady women ripped into him and, as they did, a huge swarm of flies came gushing from his throat. They streamed down the hallway and almost knocked Jim over as they exploded into the night sky. The sound of buzzing drowned out the chaos momentarily and then they were gone. Eileen and Marie latched on to Edward, subduing him in vice-like grip while Anna overpowered him in a powerful rage. They disappeared with him into the dark as Kathleen slumped against Laura in exhaustion and they both collapsed to the hallway floor. The wind died out. The music box played sweetly as Delphine pirouetted. The lid closed and the house fell silent.

Jim went to Laura and Kathleen and helped them up. They held onto each other for support as they hobbled down the hall and away from the house.

DELPHINE

EPILOGUE:

The taxi weaved through the busy traffic of the Xinhua Road and turned right onto Fazhan Avenue. It stopped by the Huanan Seafood Market and Bo Chen Yang emerged. He took his wallet and he spoke as he paid the driver. "This is Wuhan market... all or just Seafood?" The driver pointed further down Fazhan Avenue "Dongbei dumplings there ..." and he pointed to Huanan "Seafood market ... is good ... but wet market ... dogs, cats... shit." He shuddered and handed Bo his change. Bo browsed through the seafood stalls and was greeted by smiles and Chinese hospitality. Old ladies in conical rice hats held up prize crabs and lobster while tuna and snapper were being carved nearby. He walked along the stalls and, in the banter and the chatter, he could hear another sound. It was the sound of agony.

He walked a little further and stopped in the middle of the market street. Up ahead, the road was lined with cages filled with live dogs, donkeys, deer, wolf pups, porcupines, Badgers and Bamboo rats. On the side streets he could hear the screams of Fruit Bats, Foxes, Peacocks and Pangolins along with a wide range of abused and neglected creatures. The sound was overwhelming and he retreated a little in disgust.

But then, another sound caught the attention of traders and patrons alike. It grew in intensity until all motion stopped and even the caged creatures fell silent in fear. It started as a hum, like a low flying plane but the buzzing became clearer. Everyone looked to the sky as a black swarm blocked out the noon day sun and tens of thousands of flies plummeted onto the scene below. Stalls were left empty as traders took to running and patrons skipped past cages of animals in abject panic.

The swarm crawled over everything and everyone and they crept along blood stained counter tops infecting as they went. People pulled at their hair and swatted the air but still the flies got in. They squirmed their way into uncovered nostrils and gaping mouths as the throng sought sanctuary. Then the sound started to die out and, as quickly as it happened, it was over. The markets went silent as masses of dead flies littered the pavements and the thoroughfares. The traders returned, still eyeing the sky but they were reassured by their patrons who just wanted to stock up and leave.

Buckets of water were scattered over the dead swarms and powerhouses cleaned down the worktops before business resumed and live animals screamed in terror once again as the peddling continued. Bo Chen Yang had seen enough. He'd been gone too long to accept this and he yearned to be on a west coast trawler moored to a village harbour at the end of another day. He turned in revulsion and started back toward Fazhan Avenue but, as he walked, a dry cough was spreading like wildfire through the crowds... and the streets... and the cities... and beyond.

Made in the USA
Coppell, TX
09 October 2021